MEMPHIS JOHN

LESTER MORAND

Copyright © 2018 by Lester Morand.

All rights reserved, including the right to reproduce this book or portions thereof in any form whatsoever.

Memphis John is a work of fiction inspired by true events. Certain long-standing institutions, agencies, public offices and historical events are mentioned, but the characters involved, with the exception of public figures, are wholly imaginary. Names, characters, businesses, places, events and incidents are either the products of the author's imagination or used in a fictitious manner to provide a sense of realism and authenticity. With the exception of public figures, any resemblance to actual persons, living or dead, is purely coincidental.

To my mother,
who has enriched my life beyond measure

I

THIS IS GOING to be a bad day—in more ways than one, John Harrison thought. *I've already read the newspaper. I'm sure Chris is waiting for me. He knows who I'm involved with.* It was early spring of 1983 and the weather was comfortably warm with a gentle breeze. In many respects, Memphis was a sleepy, Mid-South city known for its white oaks, Southern drawls, Elvis and the "Memphis Mafia." In fact, there was also another carefully subdued Mafia presence in the city.

John, belying his thirty years, with deep-set brown eyes and neatly combed dark brown hair, was casually attired in a tan sports jacket and slacks. He paused on the narrow walkway of his River Bluff condominium to view the elegance of the deceptively powerful Mississippi River below.

Dark clouds were slowly drifting toward the early sun and would soon obscure its morning luster.

Driving to his office in his Cadillac DeVille, John stopped for a red light, aware that he was close to the Lorraine Motel.

It was there, where Dr. King was killed. Only a few people know what really happened—and I am one of them!

BIG BOB'S BOWLING and Pool Hall had been the hub for a lot of talk about the sanitation workers' strike that began with a walkout in February 1968. Workers protested low wages and dangerous working conditions following the death of two employees, and wanted a union. Negotiations stalled. On March 18th, Dr. Martin Luther King Jr. arrived in Memphis and delivered a speech in support of the sanitation workers.

He returned to Memphis ten days later to lead a protest march on City Hall. Several thousand demonstrators participated, many carrying bold black-lettered signs that read *I Am A Man*. On Beale Street, the protest suddenly turned violent as contingents at the rear of the procession began to smash storefront windows and began looting. When marchers turned onto Main Street, they encountered a line of hundreds of police equipped with riot gear.

Organizers quickly removed Dr. King from the chaos. Peaceful marchers were caught up in the same violence as youthful aggressors shouting "Go! Go! Go!" The confrontation escalated and downtown Memphis became a battleground. Police officers responded with tear gas and batons to quell the insurgents.

At the mayor's request, Tennessee's governor dispatched four thousand National Guardsman and state riot police to restore order in Memphis. A curfew was imposed. Only people with essential jobs were allowed to be out.

That evening, stores in black neighborhoods were sporadically pillaged and burned. The following day, fire companies were busy spraying smoldering buildings as glass companies replaced shattered windows. The National Guard's presence calmed the city but tensions remained high.

At a press conference, Dr. King disavowed his organization's responsibility for the violence. He affirmed that he would return to Memphis again to lead a more orderly march.

At Big Bob's snack bar, customers voiced dissenting opinions.

"No Watts in Memphis, like the riots in Los Angeles and Detroit."

"Give 'em a raise; end the strike."

"No march with a black leader."

But on Thursday evening, April 4, 1968, there was a sudden uproar of anxious excitement at Big Bob's that resonated throughout the entire building. The television was blaring. "Dr. Martin Luther King Jr. has been killed."

Big Bob's deep voice came over the loud speaker. "Everyone go! We're closing." Violence was expected.

Big Bob instructed John, his young protégé, "Stack the bowling balls and clear the pool tables—then go home."

At that moment, two men entered the building through the fire exit door and walked past the pool tables toward the snack bar. Joey Bellisario, the owner of Big Bob's, was waiting for them.

John got a good look at the two who came in. He recognized Gino Marchesino from the New Orleans crime family; he occasionally showed up at Big Bob's from time to time. There was no mistaking Gino with the ugly scar under his right eye. He was short and stocky, with dark eyes, dark hair and a demanding attitude. John made a mental note: *Gino's in charge.*

John had never seen the other man. He was Latino, wearing wire-frame sunglasses, a brown cap and brown suede jacket.

Joey, Gino and the stranger quickly headed toward private rooms located behind the bowling lanes, shielded from public view. John's thoughts were racing. *This doesn't look right to me! Everyone else has left. I wonder what's going on. Why are those two here—and with Joey! There has to be a reason!*

John, safely at home, intently watched the unfolding news with his family. As violence erupted in cities across America, the media memorialized Dr. King as an eloquent orator and advocate for nonviolence to achieve social justice, leaving a legacy of civil rights activism for black people and the nation.

Police issued a bulletin for "a young white male, well dressed" who had been spotted running from a nearby building. It was later presumed that King's assassin was James Earl Ray. His fingerprints matched those on a rifle that had been found in the doorway of Canipe Amusement Company on South Main Street, located directly across from the Lorraine Motel, where Dr. King was staying.

John recalled that on Wednesday, one day earlier, Joey had advised their mechanical operation supervisor, who serviced the pinball machines, "Canipe's warehouse should be closed while King is here."

John had overheard Joey and wondered, *Why would he say that? What did he know?*

On Sunday, Memphis' curfew was still in effect and the city remained relatively quiet. John called Joey at Big Bob's.

"Should I come in to work?" Joey was brief. "There're only a few customers. Maybe later."

John cautiously rode his bike to Big Bob's and noticed the two men from Thursday talking to Joey at the snack bar.

No one was in the poolroom. Vinnie Vizzini was at his desk reading the sports pages of the *Commercial Appeal*. He was the bookie in charge of gambling. "I'll dust the pool tables," John informed Vinnie, who looked up. "Good idea." It was then that John saw the two visitors at the snack bar staring at him.

John casually mentioned to Vinnie, "I know Gino, but who's that other guy?"

Vinnie hesitated, "His name's Raoul. That's all I know." But, shaking his finger at John, he warned, "You better be careful. Don't go asking anyone about Raoul unless you're looking to get killed." Vinnie was deadly serious.

His words stunned John and suddenly hit him. *Big Bob and Joey must be connected to Dr. King's assassination! What about me? Does that mean I'm a part of it, too? I think I am!*

PARKING HIS CAR in the office lot, John walked quickly to the front entrance of the Rawlins House, a stately, red-brick Victorian Italianate mansion from the Gilded Age.

Ascending the front steps, John was now standing before the heavy oaken door, with gleaming panes of stained glass. A shiny bronze plaque was affixed to the brick wall, inscribed with the names *Chris Spencer, Attorney* and *River Bluff Realty, John Harrison*.

John entered the hallway, heading for Chris's office, which was the first room to the right. John knew this house well.

Chris Spencer was seated at his large antique mahogany desk, working on legal documents. When John entered, he quickly placed them aside. Chris looked up questioningly. "I have something to show you. The coffee's already perked. Sit down and we'll talk."

Chris, tall, blond and blue-eyed, was wearing a navy blue suit and white shirt, accented with a crimson silk tie. He was a year older than John.

As young boys, they had lived next door to each other in a section of East Memphis called High Point Terrace. Though their careers took them in different directions, they remained inseparable friends.

John now poured a cup of the hot brew.

"You should read this." Chris handed the morning newspaper to John who, though reading silently, already knew what it said.

Suddenly, Chris voiced, "It looks like Marchesino Enterprises and their casinos might be under investigation." He looked intently at John, who lay the paper aside.

"I know this guy," said John assuredly. "He's an investigative reporter for the *Las Vegas Review Journal*. He writes a lot about the Mafia."

John looked at Chris with a quizzical expression. "I don't see anything to worry about, though."

"Maybe not," replied Chris, "but that reporter specifically names Max Massey, who used to be at Nakoma Vista Casino. He's been missing for some time." Chris looked pointedly at John. "Do you know anything about that?"

John hesitated while sipping his coffee. "Chris, there's many things I never wanted you to know," *and Max Massey is one.*

Chris' face was tense with anxiety, and he pressed on. "John, you're part of Nakoma Vista! I see trouble. As an attorney and your friend, I'll try to help you, but you have to be up front with me about *everything*."

John sat quietly. "Chris, you should know—it's time. *Everything* begins with Carlos Marchesino."

THE YEAR WAS 1978. Carlos Marchesino, Mafia Don of New Orleans, was smoking an El Producto cigar while sitting at his massive tiger oak desk, so-named because of the light oak imperfections in its quarter-sawn wood that resembled tiger stripes. With a flick of his finger, he dropped an ash into a ceramic ashtray. Carlos was a hefty man in his sixties, sporting wavy dark hair, streaked with gray. He had characteristic Sicilian features: dark brown eyes, an olive complexion and Roman nose which, though not unattractive, was impossible to ignore. Carlos was wearing a gray suit, black shirt and gray silk tie. A neatly folded black linen handkerchief was tucked into the pocket of his suit coat.

His desk displayed the usual necessities. On the wood-paneled wall, just behind Carlos, was a framed document bearing the Great Seal of the State of Louisiana, with its familiar pelican. It was inscribed to Marchesino Enterprises.

Carlos was proud of this recognition. He had been instrumental in generating revenue for Louisiana by bringing slot machines and gambling into the state. The Marchesino Family also profited. Carlos was granted a pardon by the State of Louisiana for his past offenses. The citizens of New Orleans admired Carlos for his ability to make shrewd business decisions.

Presently, his attention was focused on a developing resort in Lake Tahoe, Nevada. In the Thirties, mobsters had built lavish homes for their families in Tahoe. They were attracted by its peaceful surroundings, with pristine beaches, snow-capped mountains and the village's serenity, devoid of crowds and busy streets—and inquisitive outsiders. It was all a part of Tahoe's rustic solitude for many years.

Until the late Fifties, when unexpectedly, the FBI intruded with their dogged surveillance. The quiet atmosphere soon evaporated.

Carlos looked at his watch. It was almost two p.m., and he was awaiting the arrival of Max Massey from Lake Tahoe.

Max Massey was a successful real estate agent who had lived in Lake Tahoe his entire life. He had represented the Mafia families when they hurriedly left their estates and land acreage to be sold.

Early on, Max had recognized Tahoe's potential to become a popular resort town, and Carlos shared that vision. He contacted Max and purchased every available property.

Carlos was impressed by Max's personable approach and expertise. Soon, they had formed a business relationship.

Max ascended the stone steps to the massive portal of a beautiful Italian Renaissance villa located just outside of New Orleans' Garden District. He was entranced by the two white marble statues of lions positioned at each side of the walkway. The sculptor had not only captured their magnificence, but also the pride and strength of the beasts. The stained mahogany door held a bronze plaque identifying *Marchesino Enter-*

prises as the business therein. Max Massey had a purpose. He had come to see Carlos Marchesino on an urgent business matter.

Upon entering and being escorted to Carlos' office, Max observed everything. His sharp blue eyes were drawn to a splendid lamp on Carlos' desk, lending a decorative touch. Max recognized it as a Tiffany, laced with individual glass pieces of multicolored hues, and assumed that Carlos must be an art collector.

In a pleasant voice, Carlos welcomed Max, who eagerly responded, "I'm glad to be here. I've never been to New Orleans."

At this meeting, Max planned to project a confident image. He was trim, handsome, about forty and five-foot-nine, with sandy hair combed to conceal signs of balding. His attire was carefully chosen.

Noting Carlos' cigar, Max asked, "May I smoke?"

Carlos agreed and soon, with lighted cigarette in hand, puffing once, twice, Max became quite comfortable. With an upbeat tone, he reported, "All your properties have been sold and Lake Tahoe's development is well underway—new shopping centers, office buildings and condominiums. It's going to be big!"

Carlos nodded assuredly as Max calmly continued, "Nakoma Vista Casino is now under construction.

"However," Max paused, "there's something you need to know."

Carlos looked up questioningly as Max elaborated. "A few days ago, two FBI agents showed up at my office. You know the feds are no stranger to Lake Tahoe. They're always sniffing around for something."

"What did they want?" Carlos sharply asked.

Max, puffing on his cigarette, continued. "They were trying to find out about the sale of your properties. They didn't have a subpoena, so I didn't give them anything."

Then, with a positive air, Max added, "I think we're alright to go ahead with our plans. What do you think?"

Carlos slowly spoke. "I'll call our attorney, Henri LeBeau. Henri handles all our legal matters. He'll have some insight on this problem. I'm sure he'll advise us what to do."

Within a few moments, Carlos, with smooth words, informed Max, "Henri isn't in his office, but presently in court. He'll be back this afternoon. We'll have to put this off until after four o'clock."

Max had no choice but to agree.

Carlos then rose. "Now, it's been a long trip for you. Have you eaten?"

Max said, "No."

"Of course not. You came here directly from the airport," said Carlos. "I'll call Dominic and Gino. They'll take you to Romano's Restaurant in the French Quarter."

Dominic Di Paola was a capo of the Marchesino Family. He was a tall, blue-eyed Italian in his mid-forties with lineage in northern Italy. Dominic was dashingly handsome and had a genial personality. He dressed fashionably in navy trousers, a blue shirt and navy sports jacket, which complimented his youthful bronze look.

Dominic greeted Max with a hearty handshake. "How are you? Last time we saw each other was in Lake Tahoe."

Max graciously responded, "Yes, good to see you again."

Gino was the Marchesino Family underboss and Carlos's younger brother. Max noted that Gino was short and muscular, with intensely observant eyes. His style was traditional "old school": black pants, a black shirt and black jacket. But what really struck Max was the deep scar under Gino's right eye.

"I'm Gino Marchesino; I don't believe we've met." Gino eyed Max.

Max replied politely, "No, we haven't." After introductions, they left Carlos' office, en route to the French Quarter.

Romano's Restaurant was crowded for the late lunch seating. Ralph Romano, the owner and a long-time friend of Carlos, was affable and reliable. Ralph was big, weighing in at two hundred thirty pounds. He was darkly bearded, with black hair and amber eyes that would brighten as he greeted his customers with a "Welcome! I'm glad you're here." Everyone liked Ralph.

Romano's chefs were exceptional. Ralph expected them to be the best and constantly monitored their food preparations, demanding nothing less than perfection.

Romano's eye-catching decor featured comfortable booths and tables with colorful lanterns. Enthralling scenes of Italy's Venice, Florence and Rome adorned the walls. Piped-in music echoed the familiar voice of Dean Martin crooning "That's Amore."

Max noted that all around the restaurant, customers were thoroughly enjoying their special pastas, linguini and ravioli, served with Italian red wines. Many patrons knew Gino and Dominic, and were calling out salutations in Italian.

Ralph Romano greeted Dominic and Gino, who introduced Max. Ralph escorted the trio to their table and immediately motioned for two waiters to come over. "They'll take good care of you. I want you," he smiled, "to enjoy my best wine. It'll be my pleasure."

Max cordially remarked to Dominic, "If the food is as good as the smell from the kitchen…."

Max stopped in mid-sentence, but Dominic interjected, "Oh, it's the best!" He pointed to two diners at a nearby table, "They come to Romano's especially for Ralph's *Spaghetti alla Carbonara*."

Max smiled. "That's what I'll get."

A middle-aged man at another table recognized Gino. He jumped up, waved and called out, "Hey, Gator Man! Come here!"

Gino quickly rose and announced, "I'll be right back." Max was watching as Gino walked over and hugged his Italian compatriot and sat down to start a conversation.

The words "Gator Man" hit Max. With an inquisitive expression, he questioned Dominic. "Why did he call him Gator Man?"

Dominic responded with a sort of laugh. "That's Gino's nickname."

Max quietly accepted Dominic's casual reply and let the matter drop. He watched Gino with an uneasy feeling. There was something intensely unsettling about him, but Max tried not to think about it.

Gino returned to their table when the congenial waiters began serving the appetizing fare. They continued to fill goblets with Romano's excellent red wine. Max's earlier anxieties began to fade.

Carlos was in his office when Henri Le Beau entered. "I'm glad you're here. Will you join me with a grappa?"

"Sounds good," replied Henri.

Carlos and Henri's friendship reached back nearly forty years to the time when they were first neighbors.

Henri was of Cajun French heritage, thin and agile, with dark brown eyes. Henri had been a dedicated student, and finally, a brilliant attorney. In spite of their different career paths, their relationship remained solid. When Carlos became Don of the New Orleans Family, he asked Henri Le Beau to become consigliere.

Almost bald with a fringe of gray, Henri continued to advise Carlos, who now informed him that the FBI had been trying to question Max.

Henri, slowly sipping his brandy, looked at Carlos. "Do you remember when the CIA came to us about Dr. King because he opposed the Vietnam War, urging people not to support it? The CIA wanted him out of the way, and didn't want it to look like they were in on the plan, so they asked for our help. They started talking money, but we needed something else.

"We told them to stop the FBI from coming after the Marchesinos. The CIA wouldn't go so far as that, but they did propose a ten-year reprieve—*if* you would agree to help them.

"Carlos," Henri was emphatic, "that time is over. Now the FBI will go after *you!* They know about Max and the Lake Tahoe properties, but that's not the real issue. They see Max listed as owner of Nakoma Vista Casino. Once they start digging deeper, they'll find out that Marchesino Enterprises is behind the entire project. Undoubtedly, the FBI will go to the Nevada Gaming Control Board, and they'll have the Commission revoke the license! You will *lose* your casino! The FBI is going to go after Max."

Henri paused. "We have a big problem. Max Massey has become a liability."

Carlos puffed on his cigar. "Henri, I think I know what to do."

At Romano's Restaurant, Gino, Dominic and Max were finishing their meal when the proprietor approached them. "There's a phone call for you, Gino."

When Gino returned, he abruptly stated, "Carlos is waiting. We have to go."

The black, chauffeur-driven limousine rolled slowly away from Romano's. Dominic, Gino and Max sat in the back seat. An unmarked, brown Chevrolet with two FBI agents, parked nearby, began to follow. Within a short distance, the Chevrolet came to a sudden halt, its driver gripping the steering wheel, as a white sedan pulled directly in front of him, blocking passage of their vehicle.

Max, hearing the sound of screeching brakes and a loud horn, turned to look out of the limo's rear window to see what happened. When Max turned around and sat back, he discovered that Gino was now pointing a .38-caliber handgun at him.

"What're you doing?" Max uttered in fear. Gino, unmoved, said nothing. "Carlos is expecting me," pleaded Max. "We have business together—in Tahoe!"

"Not anymore," stated Gino. He looked at Max with cold, cruel eyes. Max's face paled; his heart was pounding.

A pathetic figure, Max turned in desperation to Dominic. "Can't you do something?" He was now sweating profusely. Dominic answered slowly, "I can't help you."

The limousine passed through small villages with rustic cabins resting on stilts rising up out of the sluggish waters of the bayou. They continued driving on lonely, country roads for a seemingly endless time to Max, who sat trembling with his head in his hands. Suddenly, the limousine slowed, turned and stopped in a secluded spot, where cypress trees dripping with Spanish moss shaded the area.

Gino pushed the shaking Max from the limousine and dragged him through tall reeds to the edge of the almost hidden bayou. Now, it hit Max—*Gator Man*—Gino's nickname!

Max lifted his head, eyes glazed, and begged, "Please, don't do this! *Please!*" Dominic and Gino had tricked him, and now were making certain that no one would ever find him.

Gino fired two quick shots and Max slumped to the ground. Quickly, Gino and Dominic stripped the lifeless body of all identifying articles. Max Massey was then unceremoniously thrown into the murky, slow-moving waters of the alligator-infested Louisiana swamp.

At Carlos' office, Henri spoke reassuringly. "We'll do Nakoma Vista Casino Inc.—a second entity—so nothing can happen."

Carlos nodded.

Henri sipped the last of his brandy and left. Carlos, while smoking his cigar, was deeply thinking. *I have to find a new owner, but who will it be?*

2

LEAVING LAKE TAHOE, passengers could see tall Ponderosa pines and shimmering lake waters, as the pilot guided LaCrosse Air's chartered silver Bombardier jet through blue skies.

The majestic Sierra Nevada Mountains seemed to create a positive mood. All the passengers were returning from a gambling spree at the Nakoma Vista Casino.

While drinking a Canada Dry, John overheard a young man, about twenty-five, talking to a passenger across the aisle. "I lost big at craps. Next time, I think I'll only play Blackjack."

The man, who was about forty, replied, "Good idea—that's what I always stick to."

Then a winner spoke. John observed a heavy-set woman confiding to the passenger seated next to her, "Here's my diagram with slot machine number two in row three. This one brought me good luck."

Several of the fourteen passengers recognized John. He quietly pondered. *Where is Max Massey? Probably killed...*

that's why Carlos hired me to run his casino. But I never should have done that!

Slowly sipping his ginger ale, John's thoughts now turned to Sister Elizabeth. *I know what she would have said.* "John, you're making the wrong choice!"

JOHN WAS A student at St. Bernard School, located on Walnut Grove Road in East Memphis. St. Bernard was an all-boys elementary school with grades one through eight, run by a staff of Dominican Sisters. Teaching was their vocation, and the Dominicans were excellent teachers. Their classes were small. Accordingly, pupils received individual attention, strict discipline and were required to study. Parents who paid private-school tuition wanted the best education for their sons—and expected them to excel academically. Their teachers were happy to oblige.

The fathers of John's classmates owned profitable businesses. A few of them had Mafia friends; their boys were also at St. Bernard's. John was among those invited to their homes.

Uniforms were an important part of the school dress code: black trousers and a white shirt. Sometimes it was hectic in the morning if the maroon tie, which completed the uniform, needed to be ironed. John would often stuff it into his pocket after the three o'clock dismissal. Not wearing the tie would result in a demerit. He didn't like wearing a uniform, but it was required.

John's classroom had ample space for twenty desks, neatly placed in rows. Large windows dominated the exterior wall. The slate blackboards behind the teacher's desk, stocked with yellow chalk and erasers, were cleaned daily. A decorated bulletin board mounted on the interior wall exhibited students' exemplary work.

Sister Elizabeth was John's teacher. She was tall, young-looking and seemed to float down the aisle in the long black-and-white habit of her Dominican order. The tight-fitting starched white guimpe that encased her forehead never revealed a strand of hair, the color and quantity of which were the subject of much speculation by her students. A crucifix hung from a rope belt loosely tied at her waist. Her round face, with big blue eyes behind thick glasses, was devoid of makeup and her demeanor serious. She walked with a brisk step and looked sternly determined when she spoke. Her classroom was her domain.

John was now thinking about one very significant day at St. Bernard School, Conference Day, when he was in the fourth grade.

His parents were dressed in their Sunday best for the occasion. John's father, Michael Harrison, was a handsome man, slight in stature with dark brown hair and brown eyes. He was a homebuilder, a hard worker and good family provider. John's mother, Laura, enjoyed her role as a housewife. She was a petite woman, slim, with light brown hair and hazel eyes, constantly busy with her children and household tasks. But the conference this evening was especially important. John and his parents had come to learn about his academic progress from Sister Elizabeth. She smiled. "You can see that John is a 'B+' student, but he could be an 'A' student if he put in a little more effort."

John was enjoying her appraisal, twiddling his thumbs and thinking, *Things are going great.*

Suddenly, Sister Elizabeth's countenance changed. She adopted a grave expression, almost a frown. "I need to say something about John."

John's smug grin faded, wondering what was coming next.

Sister Elizabeth's words were startling. "John is either going to go down a good road or a bad road. I don't think he'll ever go in-between."

Her words hung in silence. Laura Harrison said nothing, looking bewildered, but Michael quickly asked, "Why would you say such a thing, Sister?"

The nun removed her glasses and proceeded to wipe them with a small white handkerchief. "John's different." She cast a quick look at John. "I've watched you—and I know you." John squirmed in his seat but his face was expressionless.

Laura and Michael exchanged glances, then Michael immediately became defensive. He stiffened as he spoke, shaking his head, "Sister, John's grades are good—you've said so. He plays baseball, does yard work and chores at home. What more do you expect?"

Sister Elizabeth attempted to explain in a firm tone, "Each of my students has his own personality. John always knows what he wants, but sometimes he acts too quickly, without considering the consequences." Sister Elizabeth was direct. "I'm looking way beyond today, when John is an adult and has to make important decisions in his life." Sister's eyes were intense as she looked at Michael and Laura. "I hope you will consider what I have said."

As John's parents left the classroom, Laura anxiously turned to her husband, "Do you think John's going to be all right?"

"Of course," Michael replied, forcing a smile. "Sister Elizabeth is only trying to keep our son on the right path."

But had either John or his parents fully grasped what she really meant?

JOHN SAT BACK in his airline seat, deep in reflection. *Which road have I chosen?*

An announcement from the flight attendant alerted the passengers. "Please fasten your seat belts and bring your seats and tray tables to an upright position. We will be landing in Memphis in approximately ten minutes."

John immediately drove to his River Bluff condominium to unpack. Ninety minutes later, he arrived at the Rawlins House. Chris was in his office and greeted him.

"Welcome back, John! How are things in Lake Tahoe?"

"Going smoothly," replied John, "but it may be longer than I thought before there's any change at Nakoma Vista. I don't have to be there all the time, though, and it's good to be back in Memphis. Chris, I like what you've done with the office."

"I only changed a few things," he answered proudly. "I bought new drapes and that oak bookcase for my law books. I'm still keeping the old-fashioned furniture and"—Chris was now pointing to an elegantly framed picture on the wall—"there's Maggie's portrait! I like to tell people about this special woman." Chris was smiling broadly. "Although, John, you're the one who met Maggie first."

ONE LATE SPRING day in the early Seventies, John was walking downtown on Adams Avenue when he came upon a post-Civil War residence.

He noticed an elderly woman working in the yard, dressed in dark brown pants, a long-sleeve plaid shirt and gardening gloves. She was wearing a large-brimmed straw hat, protecting her weathered and somewhat wrinkled face.

John noticed how active the woman appeared for her advanced years, as she attacked weeds with her hoe. In the next instant, she was bending over and gently tending spring flowers that were blooming against the wrought-iron fence.

John introduced himself. "My name is John Harrison."

"And I'm Maggie Rawlins," she replied. "What can I do for you?" Her eyes rested on John, who smiled brightly.

"I'm in real estate. Would you ever consider selling your house?"

Maggie looked at the well-dressed young man and somehow felt that he was genuinely sincere. She calmly answered, "Of course, I wouldn't! I've lived here most of my life, and I'm seventy-five now." With a sweeping gesture of her hand, emphasizing her ownership of the beautiful old home, she asserted firmly, "The Rawlins House is mine—and with my roomers, I manage quite well, thank you!"

John's attention now centered on the many law offices nearby, all within a short block of the city, county and federal courthouses.

An idea sparked in John's head. He had an ideal plan for Maggie, if it fit her needs and she was agreeable. He began to explain.

Maggie listened intently. "I'd like to know more. Come inside."

The interior of Maggie's house belied description. There were hand-carved walnut doors, long, rectangular stained glass windows, cathedral ceilings, stately rooms and a hand-crafted walnut staircase with wainscoting leading to an upper floor, exemplifying work created by skilled artisans.

John was aware that Maggie's parlor spoke volumes about a bygone era. He observed a magnificent crystal chandelier with dangling prisms. The large room, though badly in need of painting, was decorated with dark, mahogany furniture featuring intricate carvings. John saw that a centered fireplace was the cornerstone of comfort. It was comprised of two main parts: the white-veined marble mantelpiece and cast-iron grate for wood or coal. John could easily imagine a blazing fire in the cold weather being the soul of this living room.

Soon, John was drinking lemonade, which Maggie had served on a slightly tarnished silver tray. She was smoking a cigarette, listening attentively, as John spelled out all the details of the proposed real estate transaction.

Sitting quietly in her chair, eyes wide open, Maggie stated, almost in disbelief, "You mean, I can sell my home, receive the money and stay in my house 'til I die?"

"Yes," replied John, "that's how a life estate would work."

John noted Maggie's deep reflection. He waited patiently. Soon, she began to speak earnestly.

"My husband was Arthur Rawlins. He and his good friend worked together in the cotton business, which was profitable—one of the biggest on Front Street—but Arthur was drinking heavily, and before long, he couldn't keep up his end of the work. His partner really tried to help him but he couldn't," Maggie added regretfully, "and neither could I.

Eventually, Arthur's partner bought out his interest in the company. Arthur died a few years later."

A sad look crossed Maggie's face. "The money was almost gone. We didn't have any children and I wanted to keep my home, so I rented some rooms. Now that I'm old, I often wonder what will become of this house when I die." Maggie suddenly asked, "What happens to the two older gentlemen rooming on the second floor? I don't see how I can ask them to leave now—and I don't want a sign in my yard!"

"The roomers can stay," John assured her, "and there won't be a sign in the yard. Everything can be the same while you're still living here. Think about it. If you want to do this, I can promise you, your days will be easier."

Maggie had finished her cigarette, and John, his lemonade. He was preparing to leave. "I'll come back in a few days to see what you've decided."

Maggie suddenly leaned forward. "I want to do this *now*!" Her face came alive with a new glow. "I could hire someone to help me with the yardwork—even do some painting. I won't have to worry about money! I could go to Oaklawn in Hot Springs, Arkansas—I love the horse races. Do you think you can do this for me? Please?" Maggie's eyes were filled with hope.

John responded, "Yes, I can; I have the necessary paperwork." He carefully withdrew a standard-form real estate listing agreement from his briefcase and proceeded to fill in the missing information for Maggie. She signed the contract, which authorized him to obtain a buyer for her house.

Maggie's property was located down the street from where Chris worked. John rushed to tell him about Maggie's.

"Are you talking about the Rawlins House?" asked Chris. "Everyone knows Maggie Rawlins."

"You're right," responded John. "I'm working on a life estate sale for Maggie. You have to see the inside of this house. We can go now, if you're free. I'm sure Maggie will let us in."

Maggie was glad to see them. John presented Chris Spencer, "He's an attorney and my best friend; he wanted to come to see your house." Maggie agreed and John showed Chris throughout.

Chris was completely taken aback by the home's hidden beauty, and John knew by Chris's expression that he fully appreciated everything he saw. But John was unprepared for Chris's next move as they left the Rawlins House.

"I want it! How can I do it?" John had never seen Chris so excited. He had the look of a child, hoping Santa would fulfill his longing, but half-believing it wouldn't happen.

"Chris, I'll handle this for you," smiled John. "Let me see what we can do."

At Chris' office, John carefully explained a life estate sale to him. "You might have to wait a long time before you get the house. Maggie could live for a while. That's why your price would be lower."

"I'm still interested," replied Chris.

"Can you make a substantial down payment and meet the monthly notes?" asked John.

Chris nodded. "Yes, I can."

"Well, now you have to make an offer and Maggie has to agree," John replied.

The following day, John returned to Maggie's with Chris' offer. She listened, with cigarette in hand and eyes sharp. Maggie was extremely thoughtful, then demanded, "I want to see this young man again."

After a telephone call from John, who said, "Come to the Rawlins House, immediately," Chris walked quickly down Adams Avenue. He was anxiously surmising a few things: Maggie might have rejected his offer, and John would have to try and raise it. Chris knew that he wouldn't be able to come up with more money, and it could be a long time before he actually had possession of the house.

Maybe I shouldn't do this, he thought.

When Chris arrived, Maggie was waiting. She was wearing a lovely violet silk gown, and her thick gray hair was piled high with a tortoise-shell comb. A small jeweled emerald brooch decorated her shoulder.

With a look that didn't waver, Maggie welcomed Chris as he entered the parlor. His eyes met hers.

She invited him to sit down. "I wanted to see you again."

There was an awkward moment of silence, as Maggie carefully appraised this young fellow with the sincere face and honest look. Chris couldn't read Maggie's expression, and he didn't know that she had already made a decision.

Maggie smiled. "I like you. I couldn't just sell to anyone. I wanted to see who will have my house someday. Now, when do I get my money?"

Chris jumped up and hugged Maggie. "You won't be sorry! I'll always take good care of your beautiful house. As for the money, you'll get it in a few days, just as soon as the paperwork is finished."

Chris looked over at John with an amazed expression. "I can't believe it."

John sported a big grin. Thus, Chris became the life estate owner of Maggie's residence, the Rawlins House.

Maggie had played an important role in Chris and John's lives. She even got to the horse races at Hot Springs. They both visited her often, always enjoying her freshly squeezed lemonade.

On one visit, Maggie, with a smile, addressed Chris. "There's something I want to give you."

She was now pointing to an oil portrait mounted on the wall above the fireplace. It featured a beautiful girl with long, auburn hair wearing a white bouffant dress with colorful hues of violet, seated on a swing, holding a pink rosebud. However, it was the eyes—those blue eyes sparkling with joy—that would entrance the viewer admiring a youthful Maggie Rawlins.

With an intense expression, she added, "I hope you'll keep this portrait of me."

Chris exclaimed at once, "I'd be delighted to! Maggie, your picture will always hang here in the Rawlins House."

Maggie's lifetime could have been long, but wasn't. Her cigarettes shortened her life, and she died just two years later. When Chris moved into Maggie's ancestral home, he converted it into an attractive law office, the envy of his peers who had overlooked this real estate plum.

THE TELEPHONE IN Chris' office suddenly rang. Chris answered. "Sharon's on her way."

Chris and Sharon had fallen in love while in high school. They married shortly after Chris received his law degree.

Soon, the office door quietly opened, and Sharon entered. She was petite, with blue eyes and long, blonde hair enhancing her fair complexion. John smilingly walked over to hug Sharon, then suddenly saw Janie Fox standing behind her.

Janie looked surprised. "I didn't expect to see you here!"

Sharon and Chris were both grinning. They had arranged this meeting.

"Let's go to the Rendezvous," said Chris. They all agreed.

3

WHEN THE FOUR friends arrived at the Rendezvous, a downtown Memphis favorite, Janie exclaimed, "Look at those photos on the walls! All autographed—movie stars, musicians and athletes!"

Chris quickly added, "Everyone loves to come here for their great ribs and barbecue."

When they were comfortably seated, Sharon noticed that Janie and John were sitting closely together. She suddenly asked, "Why haven't you two ever married?"

Sharon's question came out of the blue and Chris stared at his wife, astounded. It created an awkward silence, as Janie and John just looked at each other.

Finally, Janie spoke in a soft voice, "John, why don't you answer that?"

He began quietly, "I fell in love with Janie the very first time I saw her. I was on my afternoon paper route near Galloway Golf Course, when I noticed a girl wearing a blue dress on the front lawn of one of the larger homes in that neighborhood.

I rode my Sting-Ray over to see what the girl was doing. She was holding a palette of paints and sitting on a stool in front of an easel. She looked up at me and smiled.

"I was staring at the most beautiful girl I'd ever seen, with blue-gray eyes, long lashes and wavy black hair. She told me her name was Janie Fox, and I gave her mine.

"Janie was painting a picture of the Fox home—White Oaks—a beautiful, two-story Greek Revival house.

"I told Janie that she was an amazing artist and that I liked her painting, which looked like Tara from *Gone with the Wind*. She appreciated my compliment.

"After that, I always rode my bike up the Fox's driveway to deliver the *Press Scimitar*, and made it my last stop, hoping to see Janie. She would usually be on the front lawn, and we would sit and talk." John paused.

"Later, Janie and I both went to Noble High School. The football players, wearing their maroon and gray uniforms, were the big attraction. Everyone thought that Janie would try out for cheerleading, but she devoted all her after-school time to art, her passion.

"As for me," added John, "after-school activities weren't really my thing. I was usually headed for Big Bob's to play pool and make a little money."

Janie laughed. "Most kids at school knew that John worked at Big Bob's Pool Hall, and that it had a Mob connection. I have to admit, I was intrigued, and soon we were going steady."

John then added, "It wasn't long before our carefree high school years were over."

JOHN ARRIVED AT the Fox residence on the evening of Noble High's 1970 Commencement. A gentle breeze offered little relief from the oppressively humid May weather.

When John rang the bell, Janie's father opened the door. John was expecting Janie to answer, as she always did, and was quite unprepared to face Brent Fox, who projected a conservative image. Brent was a handsome man in his forties: tall, athletic and clean-shaven, with sharp blue eyes and sandy hair that was neatly styled.

Brent owned a successful business, Fox Brokerage. He was still wearing his office attire: navy blue trousers, blue pinpoint oxford shirt with white collar and cuffs and gold cuff links. His silver striped tie was accented by a gold tie bar.

There was an immediate clash of personalities as John stood there, with his shoulder-length hair, mustache, purple shirt and blue jeans. He knew he was a far cry from the country club boys that Brent Fox wanted Janie to date.

Brent, looking at John, suddenly pointed to a gray Cadillac DeVille in the driveway. "Is that your car?"

John answered, "Yes, it's mine. I've had it awhile."

Brent appeared surprised. "Come in and wait for Janie in the den." He didn't make any further remarks.

The den was a spacious room located in the rear of the house. It had several long casement windows with sheer beige curtains, burgundy leather couches and armchairs. An eye-catching painting dominated the big wall of the den, a vibrant fox hunt scene at a countryside farm.

Brent truly identified with this gentlemen's sport. The artist had captured the scene with vivid colors: the red coats of the mounted men wearing black top hats astride their horses with hounds at foot, ready for the hot pursuit of the fox.

While they were sitting in easy chairs, Brent questioned, "Now, tell me about your car."

John answered proudly. "It's a Cadillac DeVille—in great condition. When my boss was ready for a new Cadillac, he sold me this one for a really good price."

Brent was waiting for more. Before John realized, he hastily added, "I've been working at Big Bob's Bowling Lanes. That's how I was able to buy my car." John avoided mentioning that he made most of the money playing pool.

Brent didn't say anything, but John was immediately aware that his response didn't sit well with him.

At that moment, they heard Janie coming down the stairs. She quickly entered the den wearing a long white linen dress, a white beaded band across her forehead, a silver chain with a peace symbol on a medal and sandals on her feet.

Brent looked startled and very displeased, which Janie immediately sensed. She and John made a quick exit after their awkward entrance.

Brent Fox sat uneasily in the den, reflecting on what he had just heard. He was even more disturbed to see his daughter enter the room wearing "hippie" attire.

Janie and John soon arrived at their favorite drive-in, the Keystone. The fast-food restaurant occupied a white brick building located directly across from Noble High School. Its students congregated there to enjoy the hamburgers, fries and milkshakes, but the drive-thru and parking area were the main attractions.

The Keystone was the social mecca for Noble High students. Everyone would cruise around the drive-in to see who was there, or who was showing off classy cars—convertibles, especially Ford Mustangs, Chevys and Pontiac GTOs—those were the "in" cars.

This particular night, they all realized they would soon go their separate ways. Marty, one of their classmates, summed it up as he yelled out the window of his souped-up Chevy Super Sport, "We made it!"

Then there was Tyrone Jones. Tyrone was a tall, quiet, black youth with deep-set brown eyes and an earnest oval-shaped face. He would strum his guitar, playing the music of The Beatles, Bob Dylan and anti-war protest songs.

With the Selective Service System's draft hovering over them, all young men had to make a decision: college or Vietnam. Marty, with his brown eyes and curly red hair framing a round face, had grinned, "I'm not going to college. I'm going to enlist, and when I get back, I'll have enough money to open my own garage. I love to work on cars." No one knew then, but Marty would be killed while riding in a Jeep that hit a buried land mine, just three weeks after being deployed to Vietnam.

When the crowd began to disperse, Janie and John slowly drove downtown. They wanted this to be their special night.

Choosing a secluded spot atop the south bluff overlooking the Mighty Mississippi and the Church of the River, John spread a blanket on the ground. They sat together with a wine cooler at hand and relaxed, enjoying the sweet smoke of marijuana. John confided to Janie, "I've been saving this for a special occasion—and tonight is special."

They watched vehicles crossing the old Interstate-55 steel truss cantilevered bridge that carried traffic to West Memphis and spotted a river barge silently parting the waves, probably laden with bales of cotton or tons of grain. They embraced and kissed. High above shone a full moon and a myriad of silvery stars. Suddenly, one tumbled from the sky and disappeared. John knew that one day he would give a ring to his beautiful Janie. Tonight, the world was theirs.

Early the next morning of another warm day, Janie's parents were sitting on the porch of White Oaks drinking their morning coffee, Chock full o'Nuts. Eva Fox was a youthful-looking, attractive woman, with reddish brown hair swept into a bun. Her blue eyes glistened softly, enhancing her lovely countenance.

She wore smart tennis attire and was preparing to meet her friends at the country club. Eva's life was idyllic; everything revolved around Brent and Janie and seemed problem-free.

Eva noticed that Brent was unusually quiet. He looked disturbed, slowly sipping his coffee and ignoring the morning paper, which lay unfolded on the table.

Brent was preoccupied as he recalled last evening's encounter with John and his daughter. *Why had he not been more involved in what Janie was doing? When had they last really talked together?*

Brent saw John as a nice kid who had been their paper carrier, polite and reliable, and probably headed toward some decent future. Nonetheless, Brent definitely had not included John Harrison in any future plans for Janie Fox.

Suddenly putting his coffee cup aside, Brent addressed Eva with a somber look. "Do you think Janie and John are just dating?" Brent hesitated. "Or is it more than that?"

Eva, surprised by the question, smiled. "Yes, I do think it's more than that—they're in love!"

Eva reminded her husband, "Being in love is wonderful. Remember, Brent, we had to convince *my* parents that you were right for me." Eva paused. "I would've married you anyway, though."

Brent quickly asked, "Have you noticed how Janie is dressing these days? She looks like a hippie!"

Eva assumed that Janie's unconventional attire, worn by many teens, was the reason for her husband's distress. She then pointed out, "These kids are upset about the Vietnam War. They think it's a waste of their lives and," Eva added emotionally, "when I see Walter Cronkite on TV reporting about all the casualties, I have to agree with them! Too many of our young men are being killed—and for what reason?"

Brent's face betrayed a startled expression. He was momentarily taken aback by Eva's expressive words, and suddenly realized that he had been out of touch with his family.

"But this is different!" exclaimed Brent. His face was flushed with anger as he voiced his disapproval to Eva. "John is working at Big Bob's! Everyone knows that place is connected to the Mafia."

Eva reacted in surprise, "Well, *I* didn't know! Janie never mentioned it. Maybe you're overreacting to the situation."

Eva calmly added, "You know Janie. She can be rebellious. A little distance might help things cool off. Let's show Janie some other choices."

"What about a college out of state, Brent, like my old school, Sarah Brooke College? I think Janie would like it."

Eva noticed approvingly that her husband now appeared quite interested. "That's a good idea! Let's get started." However, she was unaware that Brent was obsessed with only one thought: *I want John Harrison out of Janie's life.*

A few days later, Janie joined her parents in the breakfast room. Brent was uncharacteristically calm and displayed a slight smile. He began to use every sales skill he knew, intent on selling his idea. Brent pointed to several colorful brochures on the table.

"Janie, look at these! There are so many different colleges that you can go to and decide on a career."

At this point, Eva spoke up as she handed Janie a pamphlet. "What about Sarah Brooke College in New Orleans? It's a great school."

Janie studied the brochure, focusing on majors in art and design. Then she carefully replaced the pamphlet on the table. Janie smiled at her parents. "I know you're trying to do what *you* think is best for me, but *I'd* rather go to college here in Memphis. I'll have the same opportunities and I'll be with my friends. Can't you understand?"

Brent and Eva's salesmanship was not working. Brent was frustrated. He lashed out, "Well, you're not going to college in *this* city!" Eva made no comment, nor did Janie, who had been totally unaware of her father's real motive until now.

With a defiant look, Janie got up and left.

Several more days passed. Friday morning, Janie was sitting in a deck chair by their swimming pool. She looked up, saw her mother approaching and greeted her.

Both women loved the sun and Eva stretched out in a lounge chair, applying sun lotion to enhance her tan. She looked over at her lovely, young daughter and closed her eyes, recalling herself at the same age.

Just then, Harriet, dressed in her white-trimmed gray and black maid's uniform, arrived with a tray and pitcher of iced tea. Harriet had worked for the Foxes since before Janie was born; she had watched Janie grow up and dearly loved her. Harriet had big, brown eyes and neatly-combed, textured black hair. She was not tall, but a slightly plump figure with a warm smile.

Harriet observed everything about the Fox household. The Foxes were her family. She was quite aware of the rift between Janie and her father, and was hoping that Ms. Eva could straighten things out.

After pouring the iced tea for Janie and her mother, Harriet retreated into the house.

Eva candidly opened the conversation with Janie. "You and I have similar interests. I like home design. My friends constantly call me for advice on how they should decorate and," Eva faintly smiled, "once I was thinking about going into the interior decorating business. There are times I wish I had done that," Eva noted Janie's sudden attention, "but your father didn't want me to work, so I never did.

"Janie, your father doesn't like that John works at Big Bob's because it's Mafia-connected. He was upset; he doesn't see John headed for a good future—that affects you!

"I can tell you now, he won't change his mind—I know him. I don't want your father to make things unpleasant for you, because he will. You should be happy—this is a great time in your life. Things will settle down, especially once you and John continue your education. Hopefully, John will make a better business choice.

"As for you," Eva continued, "Janie, take this opportunity to go to Sarah Brooke. I promise you'll love it. New Orleans is a fascinating city and," Eva added with a twinkle in her eye, "your father and I are giving you a red Ford Mustang convertible for your graduation present."

The next afternoon, Janie and John sat under a shady oak tree along the bank of a small pond in Chickasaw Gardens, an established Midtown neighborhood containing many exquisite homes. Surrounded by ivied walls and protected by signs at each entrance that read *No Thru Street,* it created a private and serene haven in the heart of the city.

A flock of mallards at the water's edge was preparing to swim, with the hens at the head, followed by nine ducklings paddling behind.

As two young joggers ran by, Janie and John were quietly contemplating the beauty of their surroundings.

Suddenly, Janie assumed a solemn expression. "John, there's something you need to know. I'm going to Sarah Brooke College in New Orleans."

Startled, John asked, "Why did you change your mind? I thought we were going to college together at Memphis State."

"It wasn't all my decision—mostly my father's," replied Janie angrily, "and *you're* the reason! Why did you have to tell him that you worked at Big Bob's?"

At once, John recalled his conversation with Brent Fox in the den. He quickly responded, "Janie, I'll give up the job! I'm going to college. I'll show your father that I can be successful."

Janie and John spent much of their free time at their favorite retreat atop the river bluff. The shrill sound of August's cicadas reminded them that summer's end was quickly approaching.

"I'll come home often," Janie assured John as she hugged him tightly. Despite her sincere intentions, Janie's priorities quickly turned to college activities in New Orleans. Her visits to Memphis became fewer and further between.

Whenever Janie did come home, she and John would ride up to their river bluff spot, but things weren't the same. John was beginning to sense a change in their relationship; it was cooling. Their lives were moving in different directions, and John could feel Janie slipping away from him.

Commencement Day at Sarah Brooke College was approaching. Upon receiving Janie's invitation, John arrived in New Orleans to attend the ceremony.

The Foxes, of course, had already arrived for this occasion. They were reasonably cordial to John, but he was surprised to learn that Brent Fox had contacted a business acquaintance at a leading department store on Canal Street. Janie was offered a job in the home decor department of Maison Blanchette, which she readily accepted. Accordingly, Janie would remain in New Orleans.

Janie and John's lives had reached a crossroads.

THERE WAS A quiet moment at the Rendezvous. There had been no real answer to Sharon's question about John and Janie. At this point, Chris seized the opportunity. "Well, if everyone is ready, let's go back to our condo."

4

CHRIS AND SHARON'S River Bluff condominium was a two-story, buff brick overlooking the Mississippi. Janie was impressed with the striking interior decor. Off-white walls and turquoise-blue draperies were accentuated by a white leather sofa and armchairs. A walnut coffee table held a small planter with purple African violets.

Chris had installed a Brittany wine cupboard in one corner of the living room, which featured a well-stocked bar. He was now opening a Cabernet Sauvignon for Janie and Sharon. The wine was to their taste.

Chris motioned to John. "Here's your Heineken, I'm going to have a Jack Daniel's. Now, let's all toast to each other."

Janie, with Chris at her side, was admiring an eye-catching painting. "Look at La Goulue, the famous can-can star at the Moulin Rouge. What a colorful costume!" Janie's eyes were sparkling.

Chris spoke up. "La Goulue is her stage name—her real name was Louise Weber. While we were on our honeymoon in Paris, Sharon and I went sightseeing at Montmartre. We saw this painting in a boutique, a Toulouse-Lautrec. We both loved it. Even though it's a reproduction, I had to buy it.

"Parisian vendors try to make you think that you're getting a bargain," Chris laughed. "They know how to deal with tourists—especially Americans."

John had been quietly smoking his cigarette while observing Janie and thinking about how much he loved her.

Quite unexpectedly, Sharon voiced, "John, there's something I've been wanting to ask. How in the world did you come to know the Mafia?"

Somewhat surprised at the question, John hesitated. "I guess it all started when I was a kid. My parents were searching for a country club to join and found exactly what they wanted out in the county—Bella Casa Country Club.

"At first, Bella Casa was only for Italians, but that didn't last long. The doors opened up and that's how we got in. We used to go for their Sunday dinners. Their spaghetti and lasagna were the best I've ever had.

"Mario Bellisario was the owner. He would greet everyone with a big smile and a handshake. However," John stressed to Sharon, "Mario was Mafia—what else can I say?"

Chris immediately spoke up. "Mario ran all the gambling in Memphis."

"Yes," affirmed John, "*and* the bookmaking! Everybody liked him. Remember the St. Francis Orphanage picnic?"

"Of course," said Chris. "It was always on the Fourth of July. There were decorated booths, all kinds of food, bingo and several places where you could try to win a prize," Chris smiled. "And all that money went to charity."

"Politicians were always there too," said John, "shaking hands and trying to get votes."

"Don't forget the car raffle," added Chris. "That always attracted crowds, and Mario drew the winning ticket. Some lucky person," grinned Chris, "got a new car."

John continued. "Mario had a reason to help St. Francis. He had lived there! That goes back to World War Two. Sicily was in turmoil with its Fascist government. Angelina Bellisario, Mario's mother, sent her young son to America for safety.

"When Mario arrived in the U.S., he was placed in St. Francis Orphanage. Mario always said he would never forget the children at St. Francis."

Chris grinned, "John, how about Mario and *Il Vendicatore*? That's quite a story."

Sharon and Janie added, "We'd love to hear."

John slowly began, "One afternoon, Chris and I had been swimming at Bella Casa and we were getting something to eat. Vinnie Vizzini, who worked at the grill—I still remember his snow-white hair and piercing eyes—was talking to some old compadres of Mario."

John paused. "We could hear their conversation. They were discussing Mario's trip to Sicily for his mother's funeral."

THE YEAR WAS 1946. After Angelina's burial, Pietro, Mario's older cousin, announced, "We are en route to an old inn, La Dolce. Your relatives are all anxious to see you!" Pietro bore a striking resemblance to Mario: tall and handsome, with dark eyes and hair.

Upon arriving at the inn and following hugs and greetings, waiters brought trays stacked with courses of appetizing food, interspersed with an abundance of Chianti wine. Mario observed that many of the women present were wearing black dresses and black armbands, like the one his mother had worn for his father.

One young woman introduced herself as Sophia. She remarked, "Most of the women here are without husbands, brothers or sons. I will tell you why. Mussolini and his Blackshirts destroyed our families!"

Mario looked at Sophia, with her long, glossy black hair and expressive brown eyes. She was stunningly beautiful and displayed passionate spirit.

"I have noticed," added Mario.

With Sophia's sudden declaration, all conversation stopped and the room became quiet. Several men at the far end of the table rose and crowded close to Mario and Sophia.

Speaking in a distinct voice, she revealed how the Blackshirts had come to their houses, dragging away the men and confiscating anything of value.

One gray-haired woman interrupted, "They didn't give reasons—just took our men away. People from the countryside found their bodies. They'd been shot, and wooden signs with the word *Antifascista* hung around their necks." She wiped tears from her eyes, still remembering.

There was a heavy silence until Sophia asserted loudly, "We rejoiced when the Italians shot Benito Mussolini and hung him by his heels!"

Mario boldly declared to his compatriots, "My father was killed, like your fathers. We will find those Blackshirts responsible—I will help you do this!" Mario's face reflected his determination. All of La Dolce's guests loudly cheered and joined in a toast.

Pietro now jumped up, "Some of these Blackshirts are living right here in Palermo. One is a high-ranking carabinieri; another works with him. Two more are in business—one has a jewelry store and the other is an antique dealer."

The dinner ended with a single thought—*vendetta*. Mario, Pietro and a few of their relatives continued to discuss how to trap the former Blackshirts. The conspirators then proceeded to work out the details of their plan.

On a typical noonday, the two carabinieri from the local police station dined together at a small bistro located just a short walk down the street. Being creatures of habit, they took lunch at the same time every day.

Shoppers crowded along the narrow street. Suddenly, two young men who had been waiting in a doorway stepped out, drawing guns on the surprised officers.

Everyone stared, but no one tried to stop the gunmen, who quickly pushed the two policemen into a waiting van and sped away. Witnesses recognized the gunmen as local Mafioso. There was no great love for these carabinieri, due to their reputation as former Blackshirts.

The same tactics were employed again at the jewelry store and antique shop: surprise visits and drawn guns, with no one interfering. Both proprietors were quickly overpowered, thrown into vans and taken away.

Judgment was at hand. Several parties of men drove out of Palermo to a familiar spot, where retribution was to be exacted.

Moonlight shone on a remote, dusty dirt road, revealing a copse of majestic trees, tall and gnarled with age. A stream of cars parked behind a canvas-covered truck, and two men with lighted torches stood by as the four prisoners were dragged out and lined up under an ancient olive tree before a firing squad of partisans.

These Sicilians, standing in silence, were ready to avenge their executed relatives, who several years earlier had stood under that very same tree on this very same road.

With a somber look, Pietro said, "Mario, these men must know why they are here. Our dead brothers deserve this moment. Will you speak for us?"

Mario nodded, "Yes." He stepped forward, gave each of the condemned men a lighted cigarette and loudly announced, "You murdered the fathers, brothers and sons of these men standing here when you were Mussolini's Blackshirts." Several bystanders spat upon the ground.

There was a foreboding stillness, suddenly broken by the police chief, who, in a defensive voice asserted, "We were soldiers—we had to follow orders."

No one responded. The prisoners were blindfolded as four partisans with Italian carbines stood in readiness. Mario raised his hand and gave the signal to fire. A volley of shots rang out—eight in all. Mario handed Pietro a wooden sign with the word *Fascista* painted in black letters, which he then hung around the neck of the police chief.

There was no clapping of hands, no shouts. The small crowd, still holding their torches, was waiting. Mario addressed them passionately.

"I earnestly hope that we are sending a strong message! These four men represent only a small number of guilty Blackshirts still alive in Sicily and Italy. My own country has no love for these Fascists. The families of these Blackshirts must make amends for what was stolen from your relatives. This is payback. You will have to continue the vendetta yourselves. I am returning to the United States."

Pietro now stepped forward, embraced Mario, and loudly declared, "Il Vendicatore—the Avenger!"

Mario and the Sicilian patriots' retribution sparked a movement abroad against known Fascists.

The news spread quickly to American shores. Upon Mario's return to New Orleans, he was summoned to meet with the Don, Carlos Marchesino, who hugged him warmly. "You are a courageous soldier. You've carried out a vendetta for our fathers. I'm proud of you, and I want you to be my capo."

Mario, with a grateful look, replied softly, "I'm honored." Carlos continued, "Now, I need someone like you in Memphis. I trust you won't disappoint me."

"AFTER VINNIE FINISHED his story," added John, "everyone was quiet. We all regarded Mario with a new respect, especially me. He became my new hero.

"A couple of weeks later, Chris and I were walking around outside Bella Casa. We ran into two friends who were doing a little lagging— coin tossing—next to a brick wall, out of sight. They asked us to play. I knew that Sam and Rick thought they had lucked up with two losers, but a good lagger knows not to throw his coin too hard. The coin closest to the wall is the winner. I was good at this game—and I was winning!

"All of a sudden, out of nowhere, Joey Bellisario showed up and said we were gambling and it wasn't allowed. We were scared, especially when he made us come with him to talk to his father, Mario.

"Mario was watching a bocce ball game. Joey—he looked just like Mario—told him that we had been gambling and pointed to the spot where we had been lagging. We were too scared to say a word. Mario looked us over. I knew that Joey had seen me shoving quarters into my pocket.

"Chris tried to explain that we weren't gambling, just trying to see how far we could throw the quarters." John laughed. "Chris, I should've realized right then that you'd make a good lawyer!

"Mario smiled a little and said that he better not catch us gambling again. We all promised, but Mario wasn't finished. He asked who won— and how much!

"I told him that I won seven dollars and Mario looked at me with a glint in his eyes. He wasn't going to do anything to us. I knew about the card room in the back of the club and that some of the men bet big money. Why would Mario make a big deal of our lagging? Besides, I think he liked me."

"John continued. "But Bella Casa was about to change, because of Joseph Michael Valachi."

"Oh, yeah," Chris interjected. "He was the main witness in the '63 Senate Crime Commission hearings. It was big news on TV." Chris now turned to address Sharon and Janie, "Valachi didn't keep the Omerta—the Mafia Code of silence."

John continued. "Following that, the FBI went after the Mafia from coast to coast, and was always showing up at Bella Casa, with their cars parked right out in front. A few agents even positioned themselves at the roadside entrance and asked people for their names. The members didn't like the invasion of privacy and they stopped coming!

"Mario was angry and frustrated because he couldn't do anything to change what was happening to his club. He had a massive heart attack that killed him. His sudden death shocked everyone.

"I went to the funeral with my father. The Marchesino Family from New Orleans was there—Carlos, his son and his brother.

"I wondered," stressed John, "*where were all the people who Mario had befriended?* Only a few showed up at the gravesite. Joey and Vinnie were both visibly saddened by Mario's death. They each put a rose on his casket.

"Bella Casa Country Club was sold not long after. I thought that the FBI was totally wrong for what they did to Mario."

5

AFTER MARIO'S DEATH, Joey Bellisario took over for his father.

Chris now spoke up. "John, why don't you tell the girls about Big Bob's? You spent a lot of time there."

John paused briefly and then replied, "Okay."

BIG BOB'S BOWLING Lanes and Pool Hall was located in an East Memphis shopping center, where an illuminated sign on the brown brick building featured a caricature of Big Bob smoking a big cigar. Twenty cement steps led downstairs to a spacious basement furnished with bowling lanes, pool tables and pinball machines.

The premises were soundproof, ensuring that no one in the supermarket above, at street level, could hear the activity below: the noise of bowling balls and falling pins.

Bob Drescher, the manager, was exceedingly proud of his establishment. He was tall, fortyish, black-haired, balding, and rather heavy. "Big" fit him well. Everyone who came to the bowling alley knew Big Bob, who incessantly puffed on his big cigar—a King Edward—and shrewdly scrutinized everything. His steel blue eyes missed nothing.

Big Bob knew his customers by name and welcomed them. He kept operations running smoothly, walking around and keeping a wary eye for any rowdy behavior—those individuals would soon be on their way.

The St. Bernard students came the second Friday of each month to bowl. John was a fairly good bowler, making quite a few strikes, but he ran over between turns to watch the pool players through the glass partition. John decided, *That's what I want to do—play pool. I want to be as good as Paul Newman in* The Hustler.

One Friday, after completing his paper route, John went back to Big Bob's to play a game of pool. Big Bob was helping two customers with bowling shoes and score cards.

When he finished, John said to him, "I'm here to play pool."

Big Bob looked at him thoughtfully, then still smoking his big cigar, "You have to be eighteen to play pool and," he grinned, "you're most definitely not!"

John was surprised and disappointed; Big Bob was aware of that. He recognized John as one of the students from St. Bernard's.

Big Bob reached into a desk drawer, pulled out a printed form and handed it to John. "Get this signed by one of your parents. Then you can have a permit card to play pool." He was trying to make John feel better.

When John arrived home, his mother was preparing dinner. Laura was making a chicken casserole and listening to a very earnest son, his eyes fixed upon her, pleading to play pool. John explained that St. Bernard students went to Big Bob's for bowling as a school sports activity, and that a few of his classmates already had permission to play pool. John didn't know—or even care—whether his classmates had actually obtained permission. He wanted that permit card signed.

Laura was facing a big decision, one with which she wasn't comfortable. Initially, she was hesitant, but soon gave in.

The next day, John rode his bike to Big Bob's with his signed form. He chained his bicycle to an iron post at the street-level entrance. Nobody would touch his Sting-Ray; this was Big Bob's place.

Once inside, Big Bob smiled, took John's signed form and filled out the permit card, announcing, "Okay, now you can play pool."

John immediately went to the poolroom and saw someone familiar approaching—it was Joey Bellisario, Mario's son. Joey instantly recognized John.

Joey greeted John with a big smile. "Good to see you again. You like to play pool? This is a great place to play." He now pointed to an overhead sign with black, block letters and commented jokingly, "No gambling."

John nodded agreeably, realizing that this must be Joey's place.

Not many people knew that Carlos had made Joey a capo and directed him to run the gambling in Memphis as Mario had done previously—attracting as little attention as possible; no violence or killing.

Joey and Big Bob made an efficient team. They would monitor the twenty-eight Brunswick bowling lanes that soon would be used by the union teams. These players, young and old, came equipped with bowling balls and shoes, wearing shirts bearing their sponsors' names, all ordered by Big Bob.

Big Bob entered into the spirit of competition, wearing his best blue shirt with *Big Bob's Bowling Lanes and Pool Hall* printed on the back and a caricature of his face with the trademark big cigar in his mouth. Joey's shirt had the same logo.

At the end of each season, Joey and Big Bob ceremoniously presented the winning teams with trophies and generous money prizes. Everyone enjoyed themselves and appreciated Big Bob and Joey for hosting this occasion, all while cameras were flashing.

Joey began noticing that John often frequented the pool hall. One day, he came over to the pool table while John was playing, and said, "You're pretty good! I've been watching you."

"I like to play pool. I want to be the best."

Joey smiled. Nonetheless, he was certain that John had taken in everything that was going on at Big Bob's. He advised John, in no uncertain terms, "You can play here, but you *don't* talk!"

John quickly replied, "I won't—I promise." Joey, nodding approvingly, appeared to be satisfied.

One morning, John arrived at Chris's house just as Chris's father was leaving for work. Captain Charles Spencer was a tall, lithe man with closely cropped gray hair and keen blue eyes. As a captain in the Memphis Police Department, he posed a striking figure in his uniform.

Captain Spencer knew from an early age that he would work in law enforcement. As a young boy, he spent countless hours with his neighbor, a patrolman, asking him unending questions. Charles Spencer grew up abiding the law. His principles were instilled at an early age; he had integrity and could not be bought.

Captain Spencer was quite aware that Big Bob's had a Mafia connection. Looking firmly at John, he admonished him. "I've instructed Chris not to go to Big Bob's. You should stay away from there, too."

John ignored the reprimand and hoped that the police captain wouldn't say anything to his father.

After Mario's death, the FBI had nearly terminated their investigation of bookmaking operations in Memphis. However, when Joey Bellisario took over, they again resumed surveillance.

The parking area across from Big Bob's afforded FBI Agents Dale Russell and Brad Barnett the perfect opportunity to observe from their car the customers who frequented Big Bob's.

They now noticed a boy of about thirteen, padlocking his Sting-Ray to the iron post outside the entrance.

"I recognize that kid from the Bella Casa! I'll bet he knows what goes on here," exclaimed Agent Russell. "But—can we get him to talk?"

Dale Russell was a tall man, six-foot-two in his mid-thirties, with piercing blue eyes and sandy blond hair. He wore a loose-fitting gray herringbone suit and matching gray fedora.

His partner, Brad Barnett, was in his mid-twenties and five-foot-nine, with dark eyes and brown hair. Barnett, hatless, was dressed in a well-tailored but rumpled navy blue suit, wrinkled from sitting for endless hours of surveillance.

As John started downstairs to Big Bob's, he was stopped by the two FBI agents, who flashed their identification badges. John recognized them immediately.

"What are you doing here?" Agent Russell questioned in a stern voice.

"I'm going to play pool," John managed to respond politely. "I have a permit card."

Russell continued, "Have you seen any gambling? Any bookmaking here?"

John was silent for a moment, thinking, *I'm not going to give them any information.* So, aloud with a slight smile, "There's a sign inside that says *No Gambling.*"

Barnett, in a persuading tone, "You're here a lot. You must see everything that goes on in there."

John firmly answered, "Nope, I just play pool."

Russell could sense that they weren't going to get anywhere with this kid, but Barnett was persistent. "We are FBI," and with a tone of authority, he added, "We're going to get them." John realized that "them" meant Joey and Big Bob.

"If you see any gambling, call us." Barnett started to give John an FBI card. Russell stopped him, shaking his head, "Don't—he's not going to help us." Then they left.

John immediately alerted Joey and Big Bob about the FBI. They looked at each other and took off running upstairs. John was right behind them.

"I don't see them—I guess they're gone." Joey turned to Big Bob. "They're after us." He was angry. Big Bob, disgusted and chewing on his cigar, nodded in agreement.

Joey asked, "John, did they give you their names?"

"Dale Russell and Brad Barnett," John replied.

"I know those two," voiced Joey. "The same agents who were at Bella Casa." Joey was now visibly irate. "John, they shouldn't have asked you about anything. You're a *minor*. You're not eighteen."

"I didn't tell them anything," answered John. "You always say 'Don't talk.'"

Joey paused, then patted John on the shoulder. "You did very good."

The following morning at the snack bar, Big Bob and Joey remained concerned about John's encounter with the FBI. Big Bob, puffing away on his cigar, brought the matter up to Joey. "John didn't talk. Let's do something for him."

Joey thought for a moment. "You're right." Then he grinned. "I kinda like John. Vinnie could use some help. Let's give John a few dollars to work with him. What do you think?"

Big Bob agreed. "Good idea."

Vinnie, who was in his early sixties, welcomed John's assistance. He carefully instructed his new helper. "John, everything has to be done right. Stack the bowling balls, get rid of the trash and sweep the floors before the bowling crowd gets here."

When Vinnie zeroed in on the pool table area, he pointed out to John that the cue sticks had to be replaced in the wall racks, and the pool tables with green felt covers needed to be dusted.

The job was going well. If it was a slow day with few customers, Vinnie would say, "John you can play pool," and with a twinkle in his brown eyes, *"for free!"* John really liked those days, and soon gave up his paper route to spend more time at Big Bob's.

Vinnie was the bookie. He sat in the back of the poolroom in a swivel chair at a wooden counter with the telephone, ready to take bets. A television was mounted overhead, with benches positioned nearby so bettors could watch the sporting events. Vinnie was a pro with the odds and point spreads. The money centered mostly on baseball, football and basketball, but also included boxing and horse racing. Vinnie was always on hand for the payoffs but, more often, it was just the opposite. Losers were paying Vinnie—and if they didn't, Vinnie had his own ways to collect.

There was a secluded room behind the bowling lanes that had a large, round poker table with red Naugahyde chairs. Big Bob was in charge of the card games there, which usually accommodated four to eight players—and that meant big money.

Vinnie's wife, Nina, worked at the snack bar. Nina was fifty-five, with deep brown eyes, short graying hair and a full figure. She ordered prime meats, fresh produce, breads and coffee from Memphis' food purveyors. Big, juicy hamburgers with all the fixings, fries, onion rings and the delicious aroma of coffee permeated the snack bar. Customers loved Nina's pleasant demeanor and genuinely appreciated having someone so cheerful to serve them. The snack bar was popular; bowling league evenings and weekends were the busiest times for Nina.

"MONEY ALWAYS WENT on at Big Bob's," John recalled to his friends. "The jukebox was next to the snack bar, and five pinball machines were lined up by the side wall near the bowling lanes.

"On Tuesdays, the day before the operation supervisor arrived, Joey would open the first pinball machine with a key that he had specially made for him. He took out half the money, while I held the money bag, then pushed the box back into the machine. Then he'd do the same with the other four pinball machines and jukebox. When the vendor came on Wednesdays, he only got about a fourth of the money— *at best*," John smiled.

"I didn't tell anyone. I kind of liked being in on Joey's little game."

JOHN LEARNED A lot at Big Bob's. The snack bar was usually the busiest spot. Team members constantly went to the vending machine for a thirst-quencher. Those interested in betting would place ten dollars in the pot at the counter while getting their soft drink. When the pot grew to fifty dollars, that was the cut-off. A crowd, standing around, waited to see who the winner was. If the bottom of their bottle showed that it came from the furthermost plant from Memphis; say, from Los Angeles, that person got all the pot money. Mostly, the bottles came from Atlanta or St. Louis. Big Bob had a map and ruler handy; if anyone questioned him, they could survey the distance on the map. A few wagered two or three times.

Big Bob and Joey were often the winners and John wondered why— until he noticed that Big Bob refilled the machines. He could easily see the bottles' bottoms, and arrange them exactly the way he wanted. John quickly learned how *not* to lose.

One of the regulars at Big Bob's, Greg Reid, always placed bets with Vinnie. He was a Memphis State baseball player: a popular athlete, muscular with blond hair, blue eyes and a strong pitching arm. Scouts had already been sizing him up and Greg was headed for the major leagues. He had a promising career ahead of him.

Eventually, it became common knowledge that Greg was gambling heavily.

One night, when John was preparing to head home, Greg was still playing cards. He had been at Big Bob's since late afternoon. When John returned Saturday morning at about ten, Greg was at the snack bar, bleary-eyed and tired, struggling to pull himself together before reporting for a scheduled baseball game. He had stayed up all night trying to recoup his lost money. If Greg pitched that day, the odds for his team to win weren't good.

Soon, it became apparent that Greg's performance wasn't up to par; he was on a losing streak. Rumors surfaced that he was throwing games, which became a hot topic on the local sports page. The scouts decided to look elsewhere. Greg had blown his big chance. After that, Joey and Big Bob strongly advised Greg to leave town.

One afternoon, Big Bob and John were drinking coffee at the snack bar. Big Bob turned to John. "You're pretty good at pool. I can show you how to make some money. All you have to do is find someone who isn't as good as you are—that's all it is!" Big Bob was still puffing on his big cigar.

He pointed out that Friday and Saturday nights were the busiest. Workers were ready for a little fun and had money to spend. Big Bob knew who was an expert pool player and who wasn't.

When he spotted someone that John could beat, he'd signal John by pointing.

John would approach them and ask if they wanted to play nine-ball for a dollar. Usually they would agree. Big Bob had cautioned John to lose, perhaps as often as two or three times. Then he would amble up to the table and ask, "Who's winning?" When John answered, "Not me," Big Bob would say, "I think you can do better. I'll put up five dollars." Then, looking at John's opponent, he challenged, "Do *you* want to put up five bucks?" Usually they agreed, thinking they were sure to win. Thus began the hustle game, and little by little, the bets escalated.

John had purchased his own cue stick—the finest, a Meucci—but he didn't use it until later in the game. He would wait until the money reached twenty dollars before asking Big Bob, "Can I borrow your cue stick?"—which of course was John's Meucci. Then John would begin a winning streak, splitting the proceeds with Big Bob—a tidy sum.

Big Bob was preparing to buy a new car and aware that John had an eye on his old Cadillac, so he worked out a deal with him. John became the proud owner of Big Bob's Cadillac DeVille.

6

"JOHN," INQUIRED SHARON, "didn't your father know what you were doing at the pool hall? Especially when you got that Cadillac!"

Sharon often threw out an unexpected question, so John wasn't surprised. He slowly answered, "My father knew about my car, and that I played pool." John now turned to Janie and Chris. "But I didn't tell him what went on at Big Bob's, or about Paul Alfonso, who owned several strip clubs and adult movie houses. Paul would come to see Joey every Friday afternoon around five o'clock.

"Paul was in his fifties. He was a sharp dresser and his pompadour was perfectly combed. He always carried a zippered, leather bag with him.

"His adult movie house on Summer Avenue—not far from Overton Park and the Memphis Zoo—used to be a real movie theater. You could still see the original name on the marquee. Near the old sign was a new one, flashing neon yellow and red, *XXX Adult Movies*. Paul's nightclub, Lili's Cabaret, was next door. Lili's was a popular place—people who went there felt safe.

"Paul talked about a druggie who robbed one of his club customers as he was going to his car. He couldn't believe that anyone would dare to take such a risk. Paul's security guards made sure that it wouldn't happen again! They found the poor guy dead in an alley not too long after. The police didn't seem to care about one less junkie, though, and word spread quickly among other drug addicts."

John continued. "Big Bob's had police protection with Captain Patrick Lafferty, who came every Saturday night to see Joey."

LAFFERTY WAS A handsome red-haired Irishman, nearly six-foot-five, robust and blue-eyed. Walking with a quick stride, he was easily recognized as a Memphis Police captain, with double bars of gold on his navy blue uniform and his gold-wreathed cap. Lafferty always exchanged pleasantries when he met with Joey. His visits seldom lasted more than ten minutes.

Joey's office was located adjacent to the poolroom where John played. Sometimes Joey didn't close the door and John could see him hand an envelope to Lafferty. John didn't know exactly what was going on, but later found out that these were the weekly payoffs.

All of Memphis' bookmakers came to Big Bob's with their money for Joey, who made sure that Carlos Marchesino received his tribute. This was efficiently handled by Alex

LaCrosse, who had formerly worked with the Central Intelligence Agency.

Carlos had met Alex through a mutual acquaintance and they immediately hit it off. Their friendship strengthened through the years. Alex, in his mid-forties, was tall and lean, with straight blond hair and blue eyes. He was keenly perceptive and possessed an almost photographic memory.

One afternoon, Alex LaCrosse stopped to see Carlos. Alex was in a cheerful mood. "Now that I'm no longer working for the government, I plan to start an air charter business. I'm considering Memphis. What do you think?"

Carlos looked surprised but pleased. "That's a good idea. Hope it works out."

"Now, how are things going with you?" Alex noticed that Carlos seemed preoccupied.

After a quiet moment, Carlos decided to air his problem with Alex. "My courier was on his way from Memphis to New Orleans with our money. He got stopped by the Mississippi Highway Patrol for speeding on I-55, just outside of Jackson. They searched the trunk and found fifty thousand dollars in cash. The courier was careful not to explain why he had such a large amount of money, but they confiscated it nonetheless."

With rising anger, he added, "I had a lawyer try to reclaim what they took, but it didn't work. One-half went to the State of Mississippi and the other half to the Internal Revenue Service. This *cannot* happen again." Carlos was visibly disturbed.

Alex was silent, then suddenly his face lit up. "I have an idea. Why don't I fly your merchandise? I could be your courier, by plane."

Carlos' eyes brightened. It was typical of Alex to come up with such a bold move. He loved a challenge, and Carlos had to agree. "I think you have my answer."

They worked out a business plan and the arrangement became LaCrosse Air Charter.

Alex came to Big Bob's every Sunday afternoon to collect the money from Joey that he would fly to Carlos. John would join them at the snack bar. He liked to listen to Alex talk about his travel experiences.

One such incident occurred on New Year's Day of 1959, when Cuban dictator Fulgencio Batista fled from the country. Alex and several other CIA pilots, using their Air America planes, flew scores of businessmen, professionals and their families, desperate to leave Cuba, out of Havana to safe refuge in the United States.

After Batista's exit, bearded Fidel Castro, wearing green fatigues and a field cap, triumphantly marched into Havana with his revolutionaries, where he was greeted like a hero.

While Castro was making his victory speech to an enthused crowd, a photographer snapped a picture of a white dove resting on Castro's shoulder, symbolizing the new era.

Alex recalled what happened after this historic event. "It wasn't long before Castro began making alarming moves, closing Mafia casinos, nightclubs and brothels. The operators thought that Castro would accept bribes and allow these businesses to reopen. They were mistaken and quickly found out that Castro wanted to rid his country of all Mafia presence.

"A few of Carlos' Mob friends made the unfortunate decision to remain in Cuba and soon found out they were in grave danger. All travel out of Cuba had been halted. They appealed to Carlos for help to escape. That's when he called me. Carlos knew that I was familiar with Cuba and its countryside and that I could fly into remote areas for dangerous missions. With the support of loyal partisans, we were able to rescue his stranded friends. They were grateful."

"Carlos once told me," smiled Alex, "that I always could keep one step ahead of the Grim Reaper."

Joey and Big Bob knew that Alex had been involved with the Bay of Pigs, though he had always refused to talk about it. But one day, while they were sitting at the snack bar, Alex opened up.

"It was no secret that the CIA wanted to recruit Cuban exiles in Florida to work with them on a covert mission to overthrow Castro and regain their homeland. They were able to muster about fourteen hundred patriots, and on April 17, 1961, ships carried the small army to the Bay of Pigs on Cuba's south coast for the invasion. They figured that once troops were on the ground, the Cubans would rebel and support the patriots."

Alex paused, his countenance now reflecting his anger. "But at the eleventh hour, President John F. Kennedy decided to suspend air strikes to support the operation. Without U.S. involvement, there was no way the patriot army could defeat Castro on its own."

Alex was emphatic. "The Bay of Pigs was a total fiasco!"

There was sudden silence at the snack bar. Even Big Bob seemed to have forgotten his cigar.

Alex solemnly added, "There were imprisonments and executions in Cuba. I ended up losing many good friends."

Shaking his head with disdain, Alex blatantly proclaimed, "John and Robert Kennedy deserved what they got!"

JOHN WAS JUST ending his story about Alex when there was a phone call for Chris. It was Tyrone Jones, who wanted Chris and Sharon to come to W.C. Handy Park on Sunday afternoon at two o'clock.

"What's the occasion?" asked Chris.

Tyrone explained, "We've got a group of people organizing a campaign to restore Beale Street. They're meeting around W.C. Handy's statue. I've been asked to introduce the speakers and arrange the music entertainment! Chris, we'd really like you to come."

"Sounds interesting," responded Chris. "John's in town, and so is Janie. They're with us now."

"Great!" Tyrone answered. "I'd like to see all of you."

After momentarily covering the receiver to obtain a consensus, Chris informed him, "We'll meet you Sunday afternoon."

Turning to John, "Tyrone's going to be the emcee at the Beale Street event. Quite an honor!"

John grinned. "I always thought Tyrone was headed for Stax or Motown. Instead, he decided to become a music promoter here in Memphis."

John turned to Janie and Sharon. "We knew his father, Benjamin, before we even met Tyrone. "He was our garbage man."

"I can picture Benjamin now: a big man in blue overalls, always whistling some song when he came into our backyard to grab our trash. Then he'd carry it out on his shoulder to the truck."

"Some things you can't ever forget," stated Chris. "One is when Martin Luther King Jr. came to Memphis for the sanitation workers. I remember watching TV and seeing clips of his last speech on April 3rd at the Mason Temple—the one where he said 'I've been to the mountaintop' and predicted the possibility that he might die. His eyes showed how he felt.

"You knew that Benjamin and Tyrone were with a group of supporters at the Lorraine Motel when Dr. King was shot and killed?"

Janie exclaimed, "I didn't know that! How horrible for Tyrone! I remember for weeks after, I'd see him in the halls at school. He seemed so depressed."

"Dr. King was against the Vietnam War!" Chris declared, shaking his head. "That's why he was killed."

Chris now looked questioningly at John. "You were at Big Bob's on that fateful day. You must have heard *something*."

All eyes were upon John. He drew a deep breath. "I never wanted to talk about what happened at Big Bob's, but I knew what went on there.

"Thursday evening, right after we heard the news bulletin about Dr. King's death, I saw two men come in through the fire exit door, which no one ever used. I thought that was unusual. One guy I recognized—Gino Marchesino. The other one was Latino—I'd never seen him before—but I noticed that he had his coat collar pulled up and his hat pulled down. He looked suspicious.

"First they headed toward the snack bar; then Joey Bellisario escorted them to the back of the lanes, where there were private rooms not open to the public. These were the card rooms—I wondered how only two people were going to play cards. Then Joey returned to where I was clearing the pool tables. He knew I'd been watching everything and told me to go home.

"I saw those same two men again when I rode my bike to Big Bob's on Sunday, after the city had calmed down. They were talking with Joey at the snack bar. When I asked Vinnie Vizzini who the Latino was, he told me that his name was Raoul. Then he warned me not to say anything to anybody.

They were a strange pair—certainly not regulars. Why would Gino from the New Orleans Mafia and Raoul, a hitman, happen to be at Big Bob's the same day that Dr. King was murdered? A coincidence? I don't think so! They had to be a part of it!"

Chris quickly asked, "Are you saying that the Mafia killed Dr. King?"

John slowly shook his head. "I've asked myself that same question again and again. Dr. King had many enemies—the Mafia was among them, somehow."

The living room suddenly grew quiet. Even the enticing cheese and crackers remained untouched, as everyone was astounded by John's unexpected reply.

"But," he added, "there's something else. A few months later, I was watching Robert Kennedy on TV, after he won the California primary on June 5th, beating out George McGovern. The crowd was chanting, 'We want Bobby!' He stood at the podium at the Ambassador Hotel in Los Angeles, gave the victory sign and pushed back some hair from his forehead. Shortly after midnight, while leaving through the hotel kitchen, Bobby was shot twice in the head. He died the next day."

Janie spoke up. "We were all counting on Bobby to bring our soldiers home from Vietnam. What was that assassin's name? Sirhan or something."

"Oh yeah," interjected Chris. "You're right. Sirhan Sirhan, a Palestinian with Jordanian citizenship."

Janie added confidently, "There were others involved, too."

"I agree with you," affirmed John. "Big Bob had been taking wagers on the upcoming presidential election. A lot of people were betting on Robert Kennedy, who seemed like a sure thing, so I tried to put in my twenty dollars, too. Big Bob said, 'Not a good idea.'

"I was confused," added John. "Did he know Richard Nixon would win, or was the media going to publicize something about Marilyn Monroe and Bobby Kennedy to hurt his chances of winning? What was Big Bob trying to tell me?

"The week after Bobby's death," continued John, "I stopped by the snack bar where Joey, Big Bob and Alex were sitting. Joey was holding the bank bag that Alex would fly to New Orleans. They were all in a happy mood.

"Joey casually mentioned that the bag was much heavier than usual—lots of money had been bet on Kennedy.

"What really stunned me," stressed John, "was Big Bob. I can still picture his face when he said, 'They'd never let Bobby Kennedy be president.' Big Bob was puffing on his cigar. I looked at Joey, then at Alex, who was looking smug. Alex told me that Bobby wanted out of Vietnam. That's why he got killed.

"I couldn't believe it!" exclaimed John. "They all *knew* what was going to happen!"

Sharon and Janie stared in astonishment.

Chris questioned, "Why didn't you tell me?"

After pausing, John replied, "Tell *you*, Chris? I couldn't talk about this—to *anyone!*"

7

WHILE THE FOURSOME nibbled on cheese and crackers, with drinks refreshed, there was a sudden lull in the conversation. Janie attempted to brighten the mood. "Sharon, I really love your condo. It's so... Memphis!"

Chris quickly added, "John was behind River Bluff Condominiums. Pretty interesting, Janie. Let him tell you about it."

She smiled. "I'd love to hear!"

John started hesitatingly. "First, I had to tell Joey and Big Bob that I was going to Memphis State and wouldn't to be able to keep my job. My father was hoping I'd work with him building houses, but that didn't appeal to me. He suggested real estate, which I thought was a good idea, so I got my real estate license.

"As the Vietnam War was winding down, we had a recession—business was bad. I called on a number of attorneys whose divorce clients wanted quick property settlements. That worked out pretty well and got me through those difficult years.

"I still went to Big Bob's for Nina's cheeseburgers," added John, smiling. "Joey and Big Bob were always glad to see me. We sat at the snack bar and talked about my business. Joey told me he knew how I could make more money in real estate. He had friends who did this. Big Bob nodded in agreement.

"I listened closely," continued John. "What Joey was telling me did have some legitimacy; however, I realized that basically, *it was a scheme*— and I couldn't do that.

"In real estate, your reputation is your most important asset and, after a few shady deals, there goes your name! I stressed that to Joey and Big Bob, and they understood.

"Besides," John added, "Chris and I were now in our offices at the Rawlins House and doing well."

JOHN INFORMED CHRIS, "I just talked to a man named Raymond Berger about selling his old warehouse. I'm on my way to see him now. I'll be back later."

The morning's incessant drizzle suddenly abated and a bright noonday sun began to warm the spring day. John was standing atop a high river bluff before a huge, brown brick warehouse—vacant but imposing—with the name *Berger Bros.* painted in bold, black letters. He thought, *Of course! Berger Brothers! You can buy their Ball King Franks at baseball and football games—and the supermarket. Everyone loves them.*

Upon unlocking the warehouse door, John saw the worst—broken windows, crumbled cement floors with puddles of dripping water and dampness permeating throughout; discarded pallets and trash were piled everywhere. He spotted a dead pigeon lying near one corner, surrounded with a scattering of feathers. Nothing was appealing at first glance—and this had once been the largest meat packing plant in Memphis.

Exiting the moldy warehouse and encountering fresh air, John observed a vast stretch of land before him, formerly used for parking. From his vantage point, he could see the Mississippi River below and, to the right, the *Southern Belle*, a magnificent, white, double-decked showboat with a red paddle wheel.

Passengers lined up on the gray cobblestone landing, waiting to board for their cruise to New Orleans. But John's attention shifted in a different direction—the bustling activity of downtown: traffic and the commuters who worked downtown but lived in the burgeoning suburbs. Suddenly, an intriguing idea struck him: *homes—right here on this scenic bluff!*

When John drove back to Ball King's new offices, Raymond Berger listened attentively as John requested a sales price for the old warehouse and adjoining land. Berger was anxious to sell the property and, until now, had received no offers. He quietly assessed the eager young man sitting in front of him. *Why not give him the opportunity?* Berger finally agreed on a price and John had a signed real estate contract.

John excitedly approached Chris in his office at the Rawlins House. "How about being my partner—building condos! I've heard about this new concept in New York, where it's been quite successful. They're not in Memphis yet, but Chris, *we could be the first!*"

John drew a deep breath and waited anxiously.

Chris sat back, astounded. He didn't know what to say, but knew one thing for sure: *John always recognized a good opportunity.*

"I'd like to be your partner," Chris agreed. "But," he cautiously added, "how are we going to get the money?"

William Reese III, the president of the Bank of Memphis, an institution established in 1867, listened in his walnut-paneled office as John presented their plan. "We intend to build condominiums. The river bluffs have so much potential, but we need financing."

Chris nodded in agreement.

Reese was a tall, stocky man in his late fifties, with graying hair that, despite evident balding, was neatly combed. He had deep-set blue eyes behind gold-framed bifocals and a ruddy complexion, slightly scarred from teenage acne.

Two impressive portraits mounted on the wall behind his desk bore the names *William Reese, Senior* and *William Reese, Junior.*

Reese didn't respond at once, then frowned and spoke with a serious tone. "You're talking about quite an undertaking. As a banker, what concerns me is your lack of experience. You've never done anything like this before."

Chris glanced at John, sensing that matters weren't going well. Then he courageously spoke. "That's not entirely true, Mr. Reese. John negotiated my purchase of the Rawlins mansion—then I secured a listing in the National Register of Historic Places. That's how we were able to get grant money for repairs and preservation."

Reese then paused to carefully study the two young men sitting in front of him. He knew about their acquisition of the Rawlins House, but had somehow overlooked the solitary elegance of the river bluff, as had so many other entrepreneurs—until now.

The banker spoke firmly. "You have some interesting plans. I can help you; that is, if you'd be interested in a third partner. I have the money. Together we can build condominiums on the bluff—second to none." Reese's enthusiasm was growing. "I'd consider having a place there myself."

John looked at Chris, who eagerly nodded in assent. Then John addressed Reese. "Yes—let's make it a threesome!"

Reese added, "Sell that warehouse! We'll still own the land, of course. I know the Berger brothers. I'm sure we can work something out."

Upon leaving Reese's office, Chris turned to John with a broad smile. "You did it again."

"*We* did it—you helped," John chuckled.

Dark clouds were cruising in the overcast sky. The city was celebrating its month-long Memphis in May International Festival. Hordes of partygoers congregated downtown at Tom Lee Park to enjoy the barbeque cooking competition and music entertainment. John and Chris were among them, spreading the word about River Bluff Condominiums.

A gentle spring rain fell as Chris and John headed for Tony's, a new Italian restaurant downtown. Italy's tricolored green, white and red flag was displayed outside the entrance. All around the dining room and bar, people in a merry mood exchanged greetings of "ciao" and "grazie."

Drinking a Heineken, John casually mentioned to Chris, "We need to sell our warehouse."

A young man at the next table overheard what John said and tapped him on the shoulder. "Do you mean that Berger Brothers building?" He was pointing in the direction of the warehouse on the bluff, which was visible from the restaurant.

John quickly replied, "That's the one."

The man smiled. "I'm Lou Marchesino—and I'm interested."

Lou was trim, tanned and strikingly handsome, in his early thirties, with dark eyes and long, dark hair, combed back. He wore casual slacks and an expensive sports jacket, accented by a gold chain around his neck and large diamond on his ring finger. Lou was accompanied by a voluptuous platinum blonde who resembled Jayne Mansfield. She had already attracted the eye of everyone present with her shapely figure. Her cleavage was partially exposed by the plunging neckline of her stunning red silk dress.

John addressed Lou. "How does tomorrow at four o'clock at the warehouse suit you?"

Lou agreed. "That sounds good."

John knew the name Marchesino. Nonetheless, he wanted a buyer for the warehouse and gave it no further thought.

The following afternoon at precisely four o'clock, a white Lincoln Town Car pulled up in front of the warehouse where John stood waiting.

Lou cordially introduced the older man accompanying him. "This is my father, Gino Marchesino."

The moment that John saw Gino, he recognized him from Big Bob's some years ago. Gino looked the same, perhaps several pounds heavier, but that telltale scar under his right eye hadn't faded.

Although Gino's somber expression didn't appear to change, John detected a flicker of recognition. However, Gino didn't acknowledge it by making eye contact or saying anything.

"Let's tour this warehouse," John announced.

Gino was favorably impressed with the scenic location of the building atop the Mississippi River bluff. Nevertheless, the dilapidated interior of the warehouse revealed much-needed repair.

At the conclusion of the inspection, Gino proclaimed, "I'll have to completely remodel this structure, but if we can agree on a purchase price, I'll make the improvements. You'll get your money later."

John replied in a firm voice, "I cannot accept your offer unless it's a direct sale."

He immediately sensed that Gino had expected an affirmative reply and was displeased. Gino responded in a smooth voice. "Let me think about it. Can we meet again tomorrow?" John agreed.

After Gino and Lou left the warehouse, John realized that Chris would soon be leaving his office and want to hear about what happened.

Chris listened intently while John explained. "I recognized Gino's strategy. Once, at Big Bob's, Joey told me how it worked. Their contractor will make *a lot* of repairs, then he stops working—and Chris, *we* haven't received any money but still have to pay *their* contractor—and that will be big money. If we don't pay, the property becomes theirs. As of today, there's no sale, but Gino wants to see the warehouse again tomorrow. Maybe he'll make us a decent offer."

The next morning when John arrived at the Rawlins House, Chris was waiting for him. Judging by his anxious expression, John knew that Chris was worried about something.

"I called my father," began Chris. "He's Captain of the Organized Crime Unit, which investigates the crime figures in this city. I asked him about Gino Marchesino. He told me that Gino is the underboss of the New Orleans Family. There's quite a story about him."

GINO HAD BEEN strikingly handsome in his twenties. One night, while drinking and playing poker at a French Quarter bar, two Cajuns were also present. One had a patch over his left eye; the other was bearded and burly. They noticed that Gino had won a lot of money.

When Gino left the bar, they followed him, accosted him and tried to rob him. Gino fought furiously. One of the assailants cut a deep gash on his face with a knife that left a scar under his eye, ruining his good looks.

Soon after, with help from Carlos, Gino found the two Cajuns. Pointing a gun at them, Gino pushed the men into Carlos' car. They drove deep into the countryside.

Suddenly, stopping near the edge of the thickly forested bayou, the two victims were yanked out of the car. Gino addressed them in a firm voice. "You were two against me." First, he looked at the burly, bearded one, accusing him, "You took my money." Then, coldly staring at the Cajun with the eye patch, he added, "You cut my face. That's why *you're* here."

Gino fired four shots, then he and Carlos dragged the two dead Cajuns past the mangroves lining the shore and threw their bodies into the swamp of alligators. Carlos laughed. "I think we'll call you Gator Man."

No one seemed overly concerned about what had happened to the two Cajuns, who had earned a reputation for waylaying people with fat wallets. But there were many who heard the alligator story and realized that Gino was a ruthless individual who would always exact revenge.

CHRIS NOW PAUSED. "John, according to my father, Gino has killed over fifty men! We might be in over our heads."

John held a pensive expression. "I'll talk to Joey and Big Bob to find out what they think."

Joey and Big Bob were seated at the snack bar drinking coffee when John updated them about the status of his warehouse deal with Gino. Listening attentively, Joey realized that John was in a difficult position. Suddenly, he stood and patted John on the shoulder. "Let me find out what's going on. I'll make a call."

While he was gone, Big Bob explained, "This is typical of what Gino does. We told you that. You'll be okay."

Joey returned shortly. "I spoke with Carlos Marchesino. Gino and Lou aren't going to keep their appointment with you. But Carlos wants to meet with you in New Orleans. Carlos is in the real estate business as well—and he's interested in Beale Street. You ought to go see him."

Joey paused, anxiously waiting for a response. John was thinking, *Joey just took care of things for me. I owe him.*

Smiling, John replied, "I'd be glad to meet with Carlos Marchesino."

Joey was pleased. "I'll call Alex LaCrosse and arrange for your ticket to New Orleans."

"But," Joey grinned, "we need a name for you—a nickname. How about Memphis John? That'll say who you are."

"I like that!" smiled John. "Does Carlos have a nickname?"

Joey and Big Bob looked at each other and laughed. "Oh yes! *The Big One!*"

Chris was waiting when John returned to the Rawlins House and greatly relieved to learn that they had no follow-up meeting with Gino and Lou.

He listened to John's news about Carlos Marchesino, then exclaimed with an astonished look, "I can't believe it!"

John quickly added, "New Orleans—I'll get to see Janie."

Chris' thoughts were racing. *What is John getting into now?*

8

SLOWLY SIPPING COFFEE in his office, Chris was reflecting. John's friendship with Joey and Big Bob was one thing, but the Marchesinos—that was different.

John suddenly appeared in the doorway and Chris realized that he had something urgent to share. "I've got to get down to Beale Street. I can't meet Carlos without knowing what's going on there. Do you want to come with me?"

"I sure would!" responded Chris. "I haven't been down to Beale in a long time."

Their first stop was Handy Park with its tree-shaded walkways, so-named to honor a great musician: W.C. Handy, "Father of the Blues." Its prominent centerpiece was an eight-foot bronze statue of Handy holding his famous trumpet.

"Pretty impressive," commented Chris. "His 'Memphis Blues' helped put our city on the map. Handy published that song back in 1912. I've read a lot about the history of Beale Street. Would you care to know more?"

"Sure, Chris," replied John.

"The Beale Street Historic District was added to the National Register of Historic Places in 1966. During the Jim Crow days, it was one of the few places in Memphis where black people could congregate to shop, drink and socialize. Beale became a prominent business community after the Civil War and a mecca for black culture around the turn of the century. Unfortunately, that didn't last."

"What happened?" asked John.

"Well, Beale started to decline during the Depression years. It managed to hold on until the 1960s. By then, urban blight had set in and those in favor of urban renewal wanted to bulldoze the entire neighborhood. Fortunately, that didn't come about—although many old buildings were gone. The City of Memphis stepped in to acquire properties through eminent domain. They intend to redevelop the entire area as an entertainment district. That's where everything stands now."

As they walked on, John pointed. "Chris, look at Beale! The streets are empty. The stores, theaters and clubs are all boarded up. And where's the music? Jazz, gospel, blues—all gone. Look—there's the old Daisy Theater—and over there—that's where Lansky Brothers was."

"Everyone knows Elvis was among their best customers," Chris quickly added. "Elvis loved Lansky's men's clothes—very different—they gave him his unique identity. After he became a star, other celebrities decided to shop there, too."

John exclaimed, "Look! Pawn shops! One, two, three, four, five—and over there, six, seven! All closed.

"It's a fact of life that people always need money—they came here to hock jewelry, musical instruments and other valuables that they usually couldn't afford to buy back—and not only that, those pawn shops had lots of good stuff you could purchase for less."

"Hard to believe what we're looking at," said Chris. "Schwab's is the only store that's still open. They've been on Beale forever."

"Lansky and the others will come back someday," John remarked. "You'll see."

Suddenly, they noticed new activity on the deserted street. A crimson sedan with shiny spoke hubcaps stopped to drop off two flashily dressed prostitutes, hoping for early evening prospects.

John looked at his watch. Five fifteen. "Chris, we'd better go."

Chris agreed. "Nothing good is happening here, but I guess you'll go see Carlos anyway."

At seven the next morning, with sunny, cloudless weather, John arrived at the private air charter on Winchester Road, across from Memphis International Airport. A large blue-and-white sign with *LaCrosse Air Charter* immediately caught his eye. It was affixed to a one-story gray steel building positioned in front of several Quonset arch-style hangars.

Upon entering the small waiting room, John observed a woman in her mid-twenties attending the ticket counter. As he approached, he read her name tag: *Philippa LaCrosse*. She was slightly overweight, with smartly-styled short blonde hair, blue eyes attractively accented with mascara and a radiant complexion.

"Your name?" She waited for his reply.

"John Harrison."

"Oh," Philippa said with a smile. "Wait a minute. Your ticket is here. May I take your suitcase?"

John handed the small bag to Philippa.

She added, "Alex is out on the field with the ground crew, but he'll be back before boarding time. He wants to see you."

John observed that the waiting passengers were in high spirits and conversing with each other. One young couple seated closely together was poring over a pamphlet of New Orleans' French Quarter and discussing their itinerary.

John noticed a pamphleteer box displaying colorful brochures mounted on the paneled wall. He selected several and quickly perused them. Among the brochures, John noticed two casinos—the Napoli in Las Vegas and the Rosello in Atlantic City—both of which he knew belonged to the Marchesinos.

Just then, Alex entered from the field. He greeted his passengers, announcing, "We'll be boarding in about twenty minutes." He spotted John and motioned with his hand. "John, come into my office and we'll talk."

Alex's small but brightly-lit office was sparsely furnished: a black metal desk, its in-basket neatly stacked with manila file folders and loose papers, a four-drawer filing cabinet, three gray padded chairs, and Plexiglas-framed color photographs of several airplanes that decorated the walls. "The last time I saw you, you were at Big Bob's. That was over five years ago. What have you been up to?"

"I'm in real estate," responded John, "selling property on the river bluff, building condos. I'm headed to see Carlos Marchesino."

Alex added with a grin, "I heard that Gino wanted to buy your river bluff warehouse, but didn't get anywhere with the deal."

John looked surprised. "You know about that?"

Alex became serious. "*Of course* I do," he replied. "John, if Gino had been dealing with anyone else, I can assure you that things wouldn't have ended as well as they did. Carlos must have something else in mind for you." Alex's smile was genuine.

"Carlos is my partner. Let me tell you about LaCrosse Air Charter." He turned and pointed to one of the framed aircraft. "That was our first, a Cessna Citation," Alex beamed proudly. "We now have six planes—three Gulfstreams, a Bombardier and two Citations."

"Your whole setup here is nice," John declared admiringly. "I was reading about your Napoli Casino promotion. One hundred ninety-nine dollars is a great price."

"Gamblers like packages," Alex revealed. "When we first opened, we offered this deal—and it's *still* the same price. It includes round-trip airfare to Vegas and hotel accommodations at the Napoli for Friday and Saturday nights, returning late Sunday. Guests are given twenty-five dollars in tokens—of course they can buy more. One dinner and a show with a headline entertainer are included. I used to accompany the group for the weekend stay. On Sunday, prior to the evening departure, I had already collected a percentage of what those guests spent at the Napoli."

"But," he laughed, "things are different now. I don't fly to the casino with customers anymore. I'm part owner of the company."

Looking at his watch, Alex announced, "Time for departure. It was good seeing you again, John." He added earnestly, "I know you'll like Carlos!"

John relaxed in the small Gulfstream as it ascended into the skies, knowing that he would see Janie, who had promised to meet him at his hotel.

Warm, sunny weather greeted them upon arrival at Lakefront Airport on Lake Pontchartrain. A white limousine was waiting to escort John to the Monte Christo Hotel, where reservations had been prearranged.

As John stepped out of the limousine, he was taken aback by the splendor of this *grande dame* of French Quarter hotels. The ornate baroque facade, displaying a gold nameplate that read *Monte Christo 1890* caught his eye. Red-uniformed doormen greeted arriving guests. John was struck by the shimmering chandeliers in the spacious lobby. He immediately proceeded to register at the front desk, where the bell captain signaled to a bellboy to carry his suitcase to his room. Without bothering to unpack, John quickly returned to the lobby to wait for Janie.

When she entered the hotel, he hugged her tightly. Janie eagerly kissed him, lingering in his arms. Years of separation suddenly melted away. In that elated moment, John sensed renewed hope. The spark was still burning.

Janie's blue-gray eyes glistened. She was indeed a mature woman, but her youthful beauty hadn't changed.

"I was delighted that you called. Will you be staying long?" Janie asked.

"I'm in New Orleans on business," replied John. "I have a meeting at three this afternoon, but I should be finished early. I hope we can plan for dinner and an evening together."

Janie warmly responded, "That sounds wonderful! But do you have time now? We could walk around the French Quarter—see the sights."

John was most agreeable.

Strolling along the narrow cobblestone streets of the French Quarter, they heard the clip-clop of hooves as a horse-drawn carriage—a calèche—rolled by, gaily decorated with colorful ribbons and bells. The driver, wearing a top hat and tuxedo, held the reins and sat upright as a young couple leaned close together in the carriage. Janie whispered to John, "They look so happy."

A little further down, the squeaky music of a hurdy-gurdy became louder as a group of spectators crowded around an elderly, whiskered Cajun man with unkempt, long gray hair. His wizened face was wreathed in a big smile directed to his audience.

He poured out a familiar Neapolitan melody, "Santa Lucia"; however, the crowd was more captivated by the small, white-faced Capuchin monkey perched on his shoulder, clad in a red velvet suit and matching beret. As onlookers held out coins, the little monkey's beady black eyes blinked rapidly as he extended his paws for handouts.

John gave Janie several quarters for the little monkey, who shook his head as if to say "Thank you." John noticed how much Janie enjoyed this, and they were both hesitant to leave this playful scene.

Walking further, they were attracted to a fence artist who had set up his stool and easel on the sidewalk. He was using charcoals to sketch a young woman of about twenty. Janie was intrigued by the artist's talent. "Oh, look," she whispered. "He's capturing an excellent likeness, don't you think?"

But John was observing the young woman's beau, whose face bore an intense expression of love in his eyes. John pondered, *Why did Janie and I let so many precious years slip away?*

As they headed back toward the hotel, Janie pointed to a small outdoor café. "The Café Du Monde—this is one of my favorite places! We can't leave the French Quarter without stopping here."

Seated on stools at a round table under a shady green canopy, they ordered café au lait and hot beignets coated with powdered sugar, savoring every bite.

John cherished his midday excursion with Janie after such a long separation. He decided that this was the opportune moment to ask, "Janie, why didn't you come back to Memphis?"

She paused. "Well, at first, I thought about coming back, but nothing would have changed with my father. I stayed in New Orleans so I could find my own identity. Don't you understand, John?"

He nodded. "I do; I just wanted to hear it from you."

Janie smiled. "I'm enjoying my life here. I have a good job at Maison Blanchette and a comfortable apartment, not far from Canal Street."

"What about you?" questioned Janie.

"I'm in real estate," John responded with a confident air, "but you know Memphis. The city needs to grow! That's why I'm here, on business."

Then, looking at his watch, he reluctantly added, "It's getting close to three o'clock and I'm supposed to be at the Monte Christo Hotel for an appointment."

Quite unexpectedly, Janie asked, "Who are you meeting?"

John had purposely avoided mentioning his prospective client's name, but Janie's sudden question caught him off guard. He answered, "Carlos Marchesino."

Janie's eyes widened in amazement. "I know that name! Everyone in New Orleans does. Why are you seeing *him*?"

John cautiously hedged his response. "A possible business transaction in Memphis."

Janie was elated, "I'd love to meet Mr. Marchesino. Can I come with you to the Monte Christo? I'll only stay a minute."

John was hesitant, then agreed. After all, Janie's request seemed simple enough.

Seated next to a window in the Monte Christo's lobby, John and Janie spotted a chauffeur-driven, black Lincoln Continental as it pulled up. Two well-dressed young men got out and walked into the hotel.

Looking around, the first man approached them, inquiring, "Are you Memphis John?"

Nodding his head, John acknowledged, "Yes, that's me."

The young man continued. "I'm Nicolò Marchesino. You can call me Nicky." Nicky was dapper and handsome, with dark brown eyes, curly jet-black hair and an olive complexion. He was attired in an expertly tailored navy blue suit, white shirt and red-and-navy tie.

"My father, Carlos, has requested that I meet you," stated Nicky. "This is my associate, Dominic Di Paola."

Dominic acknowledged the introduction with a firm handshake and a smile.

Nicky's attention turned to Janie as he approvingly asked, "And who is this charming lady?"

"Ms. Janie Fox."

Nicky took Janie's hand and kissed it. Her eyes sparkled. John could see that Janie was thrilled at meeting *the* Nicky Marchesino and swept into the spell of his attention.

Nicky then disclosed to Janie the reason for his presence. "John and I have some business to discuss with my father.

Will you excuse him until later?" Janie nodded agreeably, then turned to John. "I'll see you this evening."

En route to the Marchesino office in the lavishly equipped stretch limousine, with the tenor voice of Luciano Pavarotti quietly resonating from the stereo, Nicky addressed John. "Would you care for something to drink?" John declined and Nicky continued. "Your friend, Janie, is a beautiful woman. Did she accompany you from Memphis?"

"Janie lives here in New Orleans," replied John. "We've been friends since we were kids."

Dominic displayed a revealing smile, aware that Nicky was impressed with Janie.

The Lincoln approached the Garden District, lined with oak-shaded trees and a diverse mix of homes. The driver stopped at Marchesino Enterprises.

Upon entering the waiting room, Nicky informed John, "I'll tell my father you've arrived." Then, accompanied by Dominic, he left the room.

The receptionist, Tina, greeted John cordially. She was a petite brunette in her mid-twenties, with luxurious, dark hair, swept back and fastened with a silver barrette. Her brown eyes, slightly mascaraed, gave her a soft look. Attired in a stylish gray suit and white V-neck silk blouse, Tina was strikingly attractive.

In a pleasant voice, she addressed John. "I made your reservations at the Monte Christo. Are they satisfactory?"

"Very nice," answered John.

"And," Tina added, "You can call me if you need to go anywhere. I can arrange for a limo."

"I certainly do thank you." John smiled, thinking, *Why is everyone so accommodating? They must need something.*

When the intercom buzzer sounded, Tina motioned to John, "I'll escort you to Mr. Marchesino's office."

Upon entering, Nicky introduced John to his father and Tina quietly left the room.

With a broad smile, Carlos reached out to shake hands. "John, have a seat. I understand that Joey Bellisario and Bob Drescher think very highly of you."

"I've known them a long time."

"I also understand," added Carlos, "that you knew Mario Bellisario."

"Yes," replied John, "from Bella Casa. I really liked him."

Carlos nodded, smoking his cigar. "Now, let's talk about why you're here. I want to buy Beale Street. I can do for Beale what we've done to make the French Quarter the attraction it is today."

Leaning forward and looking directly at John, "I think you can help me."

"I hope I can," John responded.

Carlos was candid. "The Marchesino name can't be mentioned, but I'll step in later. We need a Memphis real estate agent to negotiate the entire sale."

Aha! John realized. *Now I know what they want!*

"Get a figure for Beale Street that the City of Memphis will accept," directed Carlos. "You'll make good money. When you have their answer, call Nicky."

John quickly replied, "Yes, sir; I'll do that."

Carlos then turned to Nicky. "Will you and Dominic give John a tour of the French Quarter, so he can see our input?"

Nicky agreed.

9

THE LINCOLN CONTINENTAL rolled down New Orleans streets, past stately homes, spreading oak, willow and palm trees, and the famous red streetcars on St. Charles Avenue—the world's oldest operating streetcar line. "They've been running here nonstop since 1835," Nicky said proudly. "Now we're on Canal Street, the city's main artery, and about to enter the French Quarter.

"Around 1770, the original city of New Orleans was only seven blocks wide, from the Mississippi River to Rampart Street." Nicky was well-versed in the history of New Orleans' French Quarter.

As they cruised down narrow streets, Nicky drew their attention to several well-known restaurants: Antoine's, The Court of Two Sisters and Galatoire's; and two famous nightclubs: Pat O'Brien's and Maison Bourbon.

Dominic pointed out several Marchesino adult entertainment clubs. "They all feature topless dancers, transvestites and male strippers."

After parking, Nicky turned to John. "This is The Bourbon Burlesque. You have to see it."

The black sign with changeable pink and yellow fluorescent letters advertised the star performers. Standing in front, a barker in a black tuxedo, microphone in hand, was urging onlookers to enter the club, loudly announcing, "Sexy girls! Everything desirable!" Nicky and Dominic escorted John inside.

The Bourbon Burlesque had attracted a small crowd for the afternoon happy hour. The proprietor, Bruno Giovanetti, immediately spotted them and greeted Nicky and Dominic with hugs. Bruno was fifty-six, husky and stood five-foot-ten. As he approached, his burly hands and aquamarine jacket exuded the aroma of Old Spice. His loud voice carried a heavy Cajun accent.

"John is here at our invitation," Nicky announced. "Carlos is working with him on a project in Memphis."

Bruno appeared impressed and led his visitors to a table near the stage. Nicky commented to Bruno, "I like the way you run things here."

Bruno, looking pleased, signaled a waiter to their table. "Take good care of my guests. See that they have everything they want."

As they settled in, the spotlight turned on the emcee, a man of about forty. Sporting a mustache and goatee, his brown hair was styled short and his sunken eyes darkly circled. Microphone in hand and perspiring profusely, he attempted to command his audience's attention by telling a few smutty jokes to lighten the mood of the crowd.

John was thinking, *That guy doesn't look right. I'll bet he's on something.*

The emcee faded into the background as colorful strobe lights centered on the club's featured star, Crystal, a graceful figure with wavy blonde hair. She was wearing a G-string for her striptease. Her big breasts, covered with sequined tassels, shook as she twirled seductively. Male customers rushed to the stage to give her tips.

Smiling, Bruno leaned over to address John. "Crystal and all of my girls are drawing cards for my business, especially at Mardi Gras. Have you ever been here for Mardi Gras?"

"I've only been here once," replied John, "but not for Mardi Gras."

"Well," added Bruno, "Let me tell you about it. '*Laissez les bons temps rouler*,'" he quoted, smiling. "New Orleans is a carnival city for two weeks. Secret societies, big parties. Purple, green and gold everywhere—Mardi Gras colors. Decorated floats with kids throwing beads, shells and candy into the crowd." Bruno's enthusiasm was growing. "Marching bands, parades—especially Rex, the biggest one. French Quarter bars are packed on Fat Tuesday."

Bruno grinned. "John, you should come here for Mardi Gras. I guarantee you'll have a good time."

John nodded. "I'd like to do that."

Bruno then rose from the table. "I have to get back to work. I hope you enjoy your time in New Orleans." He briskly walked away.

Soon the spotlight was on a new stripper as more customers entered the Bourbon Burlesque.

Nicky and Dominic's affable comments kept the conversation light, until Nicky looked abruptly at John. "Carlos sees a lot of possibilities for Beale Street. Keep in mind what he's done in the French Quarter. There's something for everyone—gourmet restaurants, bistros, boutiques, night life, sex clubs.... Tourists love it!"

Nicky paused, waiting for John's reaction.

John took a deep breath. "If Carlos plans to open sex clubs on Beale Street, I can tell you right now, there wouldn't be any deal. Memphis is in the heart of the Bible Belt and the City Council would never allow that to happen."

Nicky nodded. "John, for now, you just need to get a figure from the city. Then Carlos has a plan." He glanced shrewdly at Dominic. "First, restaurants, shops, bars and music to revitalize downtown. When the city sees how we can turn Beale into a money machine, they'll be more receptive to our wishes. Over time, we add one sex club, then another. That way, we can slip them in without attracting too much attention."

"I understand," replied John, adopting a subdued tone. "I'll see what I can do."

Upon leaving the Bourbon Burlesque, Nicky announced, "We'll drop you off at the Monte Christo Hotel. Do you have any plans for tonight?"

"I'm going to see Janie Fox," smiled John. "I'm looking forward to that."

Nicky exchanged glances with Dominic, then proposed, "I would like to take you and Miss Fox to a very elite restaurant in the French Quarter for dinner this evening. That is, if you will allow me to do so."

John had wanted every moment with Janie for himself, but couldn't ignore Nicky's gracious request. John also realized that Janie would be thrilled by the invitation.

Nicky was pleased when John accepted.

Janie and John were waiting in the lobby of the Monte Christo when Nicky arrived, accompanied by Dominic. Janie was simply but elegantly clad in a low-cut white silk evening gown. With little makeup, luminous eyes and glossy, black hair that fell to her shoulders in soft waves, Janie was the true embodiment of a Southern belle. Nicky intently admired her grace.

Janie thoroughly enjoyed riding in the luxury limousine. Nicky cordially asked her, "Have you ever been to the Le Saint Clair?"

"No," answered Janie, "but I've heard that it's the most famous restaurant in the French Quarter."

Nicky smiled. "Tonight, you will be their guest."

Janie's face brightened with excitement, revealing her infatuation with the handsome Nicky Marchesino.

Le Saint Clair's elegant dining room was the ideal venue for an unforgettable evening, where cuisine noted for excellence would be served. Nicky was the consummate host. The maitre d'hotel, a middle-aged man suitably attired in formal wear—black tuxedo, white shirt, black bow tie and white gloves—knew Nicky Marchesino. He quickly ambled to their table to present the bill of fare and recommend the house specialties. "Tonight we have *Tournedos aux Champignons*, beef tenderloin steak with mushrooms, *Rôti de veau avec pommes de terre duchesse*, roast veal with piped potatoes, and *Coquille Saint-Jacques*, a dish of scallops and mushrooms in wine sauce, baked in shells."

"What is your preference, Ms. Fox?" Nicky graciously asked.

Janie replied, "I think I'd like *Rôti de veau avec pommes de terre duchesse*."

Nicky was pleasantly surprised by Janie's flawless French pronunciation.

"Where did you learn to speak French?" Nicky asked.

"At Sarah Brooke," smiled Janie, appreciative of Nicky's compliment. "I took a few classes of French—Parisian French."

Table conversation was lively as the diners enjoyed their gourmet entrées. An attentive steward was refilling their wine glasses when Nicky asked Janie, "What are you doing here in New Orleans?"

Janie responded, pleased with the attention. "Right now, I'm working at Maison Blanchette in the Home Decor department, but someday I want to open my own interior design business."

Janie's face glowed brightly and Nicky said, "I see you have high goals. We might have something you'd like to do. Dominic, what do you think?"

Dominic realized what Nicky had in mind and was keenly aware of Nicky's growing interest in this young lady. Without hesitation, he explained. "Miss Fox, I have a friend, April Giovanetti, who has a house on La Rue Dauphine that needs redecorating. Would you take a look at it? I can make the arrangements."

"I'd love to meet your friend and see the house," Janie responded enthusiastically.

Nicky turned to John. "You met Bruno Giovanetti this afternoon at his club. He's April's father."

John nodded with acknowledgment. "Yes."

After cognacs and small talk, dinner was over. When Nicky and Dominic dropped John and Janie at the Monte Christo Hotel, John was relieved to be alone with Janie at last. He had hoped to share dinner and a quiet evening with her, but Nicky had thwarted those plans.

John couldn't help observing Nicky's zealous interest in Janie and his eagerness to promote her interior design aspirations. John pondered the evening's events. *Where will this attraction go? Should I try to stop it? Is there anything I can do?*

Janie, still excited about dinner with Nicky, was now comfortably stretched out on the multicolored taffeta duvet covering the four-poster bed that dominated their luxurious hotel room.

She suddenly reached up and kissed John. "I can't believe this. Nicky and Dominic are so nice. I'm glad you introduced me. I do hope that Dominic will arrange that appointment."

Her eyes bright with excitement, Janie noticed that John was silent. "You haven't said a word, John. Can't you see that this is a huge opportunity for me?"

John hugged her tightly. "Please, Janie, I'm asking you to not get involved with the Marchesinos. You don't know what you're getting into."

Janie, expecting John's approval, was disappointed. With a strained smile and disapproving tone, she countered, "Well, obviously *you're* working with them. I want this—it's *my* chance."

She tossed her hair aside, smiling sweetly. "Surely we're not going to argue and spoil our night together."

John knew that Janie's will was unshakeable. She had already made up her mind and continuing this conversation was pointless.

Suddenly there was a soft knock on the door. When John opened, a smiling waiter entered, wheeling a cart that held a silver ice bucket encasing a chilled bottle of Dom Perignon champagne and two crystal-stemmed flute glasses. Bowing, he quickly made his departure.

Janie unfolded the enclosed note: *To our new friendship. –Nicky.*

Upon returning to Memphis, John met Chris at his office. Over a morning cup of coffee, he shared the details of his meeting with Carlos in New Orleans, including Marchesino's architect's conceptual plan for Beale Street.

Chris listened attentively. "I agree. Beale Street could do really well with some New Orleans flavor."

John added, "You can be in on this, Chris. We'll need an attorney."

"I'd be glad to work with you," Chris replied eagerly, "but you'll have to present your proposal to the Memphis City Council and Anne Askew, the Chairperson. I've met her." He shook his head and grinned. "She's a tough one."

Several days later, John and Chris entered Anne Askew's office. Her executive desk was centered in an ample-sized room, with wall-to-wall beige carpeting and comfortable chairs, richly upholstered in maroon velveteen and stylishly arranged. A framed commendation was prominently displayed on the wall. Prior to becoming Chairperson, she had held long-standing tenure as the senior council member. Her opinions were widely respected.

The Madame Chair, in her early seventies, was sharp, intelligent and intensely interested in the issues concerning her city. Her gray hair was pulled back in a bun. Through her horn-rimmed glasses, clear blue eyes carefully observed the two gentlemen sitting before her, as she continued her characteristic knitting with colorful yarn.

John introduced himself as the owner of River Bluff Realty and Chris as a Memphis attorney. Anne was quite aware that banker William Reese had partnered with them to develop condominiums on the river bluff.

John proceeded to present their proposal to purchase Beale Street from the city, along with the architect's conceptual plan, which reflected the French Quarter influence.

John spoke courteously. "River Bluff Realty would be the buyer of Beale Street—with private New Orleans funds."

"Ms. Askew, Memphis is the capital of the Land of Cotton. I'm suggesting that cotton, as a theme, should be revived. There could be a week in May dedicated to King Cotton and Court, a Maid of Cotton, a Cotton Makers' Jubilee, colorful floats and parades—that would once again attract people to Downtown Memphis and Beale Street."

Adjusting her bifocals, Anne carefully examined the architect's rendering. She was reflecting on a previous attempt by Louisiana attorney Henri Le Beau to purchase Beale Street. She had made a trip to New Orleans to evaluate his proposal and soon found out about the sex clubs. The issue was quickly settled when Anne discovered that the real buyer was Carlos Marchesino. She adamantly refused to recommend approval of their offer to the City Council.

Anne now carefully studied her two visitors, who were awaiting her response. Intuition told her that "private New Orleans funds" had a very familiar ring.

Anne asserted, "I see too many similarities to the French Quarter. That won't play well on Beale Street."

John guardedly side-stepped Anne's statement, responding, "This proposal only *illustrates* the French Quarter to show how successful Beale Street could be."

Anne paused before addressing John and Chris. "This offer from New Orleans isn't the first one we've turned down." John looked at her, somewhat shocked. Anne's eyes held a determined look. "I'm sorry, but I cannot help you now."

Softening a little, she smiled. "I realize that Beale Street is an unpolished gem and could shine brightly with some effort. Beale could be a cultural tribute to both black and white citizens, but *Memphians* must do it. Beale Street has to retain its *own* character, just as New Orleans does."

Anne looked at her watch. "Now I have an appointment with the City Council. Excuse me." Her concluding remark informed John and Chris that the meeting was over.

Back at the Rawlins House, John looked at Chris with a quizzical expression and frowned. "Did you hear Anne Askew? It sounds like Carlos already tried to buy Beale Street."

Chris shook his head, "John, I'm sorry you lost the sale—at least you tried. But maybe it's for the best."

John then informed Nicky that the City of Memphis wouldn't consider an offer for Beale Street. Nicky didn't seem surprised and responded in an easygoing manner. "I thought this might happen. I'll inform Carlos, John. Perhaps we'll call you again."

"I DIDN'T GET Beale Street," John smiled, looking at Janie, "but I got to see you. After that, the Berger warehouse sold, and Chris, Reese and I built these condominiums."

Sharon quickly added, "We love our condo!"

The evening was growing late. John quietly asked, "Janie, do you want to spend the night at my place?"

Relaxing on the patio of John's condominium, Janie smiled dreamily. "I remember when you and I would come to this same bluff. We'd watch the river, the stars, the moon...."

After a quiet moment, John said, "I only had one thought in mind, Janie—that one day you'd be here with me."

The hot tub was now bubbling and Janie, gracefully bare, slipped into the swirling waters with John. They kissed tenderly and embraced, sharing an almost forgotten intimacy.

10

SATURDAY MORNING FOUND John drinking a cup of dark roast coffee as he watched the slow moving waters of the Mississippi from his living room window. Janie silently slipped into the chair next to him. She was clad in her white terrycloth robe, towel-drying her hair; her face, makeup-less, was strikingly beautiful. John noted Janie's contentment and immediately brought her a cup of the steaming brew.

Looking around, Janie smiled. "Your condo's so comfortable—and I like it!"

She suddenly walked over to a picture hanging above the mantle. *White Oaks* was written at the bottom, with the signature *Janie Fox*.

"You kept it, John." Janie, in a gentle voice, "I gave you that painting because you told me that I was a wonderful artist." Her eyes were happily reflective, but only for a brief moment.

Janie quickly changed the subject. "I want you to come with me to my father's retirement party."

"Why is your father retiring?" asked John.

Janie was thoughtful. "My father could always look ahead. All the banks are competing in the same business now. He sold his firm to William Reese with the Bank of Memphis."

"Tonight's going to be a big deal for him *but*," Janie hesitated, "my job in New Orleans might come up unexpectedly. I've avoided mentioning anything about Marchesino Enterprises or my apartment, but you can be sure my father knows—and that worries me."

"Yes," agreed John. "He probably does. Of course I'll come with you."

Janie leaned over and tenderly kissed him.

That afternoon, as Janie and John drove up the driveway of the Fox estate, Janie observed the beauty of the landscaped yard, with its yellow buttercups, purple morning glories and songbirds twittering in the spreading branches of a large white oak.

She was remembering her happy childhood at White Oaks.

Harriet answered the door and eagerly greeted them. "You're home!" She excitedly hugged Janie, her face beaming with delight.

Seeing John, the maid broke into a beaming smile. "And John! It's so nice to see you!" She was delighted to see them together.

"Why don't you move back home?" Harriet pleaded to Janie. "We miss you!"

"I've been busy working," smiled Janie, and Harriet shook her head sadly; she knew that Mr. Brent was the real reason.

Just then, Eva Fox appeared.

"Janie, you look wonderful." Eva embraced her daughter and gave her a kiss. "You must be having a great time in New Orleans."

"Indeed I am," replied Janie, who looked happy and chic in her pale blue chiffon gown, her hair tumbling in soft waves and eyes sparkling.

Janie now admired her mother: gracefully attractive with her lustrous, auburn hair only slightly gray. Eva was elegantly attired for the party, wearing a turquoise cocktail dress accented with a silver bracelet and pearl necklace.

Turning to John, Eva said blithely, "It's great to see you again! I'm delighted you're here!" Her blue eyes shone brightly. "I understand you've been doing well."

"Thank you," replied John. "I've been working hard."

"The patio bar is set up," Eva announced. "If you'd like something to drink, just ask the bartender."

John, aware that Eva wanted a private moment with her daughter, said, "I'll go to the bar and let you two visit."

As he walked away, Eva excitedly asked, "Janie, tell me about *everything*!"

"I love New Orleans," Janie quickly answered, "and I truly enjoy interior design."

"I'm glad to hear that, and I want to know more but," Eva shook her head, "I see the caterers motioning to me. We'll talk later. Your father's in the den and he's anxious to see you."

Janie joined John at the patio bar as he enjoyed a Heineken. She asked for a dry Chablis. After several moments, drinks in hand, she abruptly said, "Let's go see my father."

Upon entering the den, Brent Fox's face lit up. He enthusiastically rose from his easy chair and hugged Janie tightly. He was reasonably cordial to John. Brent then addressed William Reese. "You know Janie and John?"

"Of course I do," Reese said, looking at Janie. "I've known you since you were a baby! I hear you're living in New Orleans now."

Janie answered, "Yes, that's true."

Reese extended his hand to John. "I haven't seen you in a while. How do you like your condo on the bluff?"

"It's everything I hoped it would be," smiled John.

Reese turned to Brent. "John had vision. We were the first developers to build condos on the river bluff, and they're now a buyer's windfall. John also helped me get in on a deal in Lake Tahoe. Would you like to hear about it?"

Brent couldn't say no. "Of course I would," he replied, recalling his friend's adventurous spirit from their college years.

"A while back," began Reese, "I made several trips to Lake Tahoe and stayed at the Cal Neva, Frank Sinatra's casino hotel—a magnificent resort. I mingled with the tourists. Often, celebrities arrived—John Kennedy, Marilyn Monroe, the Rat Pack, of course—and many others.

"It was common knowledge that some of the guests had Mafia connections; notably, Sam Giancana. Eventually, that gave the Nevada Gaming Control Board a reason to suspend Sinatra's casino license; after that, business at the Cal Neva went down quickly. Eventually, Sinatra sold his interest." Reese paused reflectively. "However, I hold good memories of the place."

"Recently, I learned there were properties for sale in Lake Tahoe at fairly reasonable prices but, as a Memphis banker, it wasn't in my best interest to travel there just to invest in real estate—especially since I knew the properties were Mafia-owned."

With a broad smile, Reese now addressed John. "That's when I called you to represent me at a sales meeting in Lake

Tahoe. I trusted your expertise—and you didn't disappoint me."

Turning to Brent, "Have John tell you more about the convention."

Before John could answer, Harriet entered the room with a tray of highballs for Reese and Brent. Taking a sip, Reese exclaimed, "Very good! Thank you, Harriet." Brent nodded in agreement.

They had no idea what Harriet was thinking. *Ms. Eva wants to be sure nothing will spoil tonight. Maybe that extra jigger of Jack Daniel's will help!*

Brent politely addressed John. "That Lake Tahoe convention—I'd still like to hear about it."

"Well," replied John, "the first thing I found out was that Tahoe is a Native-American word meaning 'big water'; and the view—well, I can't begin to describe its beauty.

"After checking into the hotel, I went to the convention hall which was already filled with wealthy guests. We took our seats at a long conference table.

"At two o'clock, Max Massey, the chairperson, walked to the front of the room and introduced himself." John grinned. "He looked like the perfect salesman, impeccably attired.

"Max used his pointer to show details of a three-dimensional miniature model mounted on a wide table. He had dioramas of a casino, shopping center, office buildings and condominiums. Max pointed out one miniature, announcing that it would be his new casino, Nakoma Vista. Then he advised all of us to purchase property in Lake Tahoe.

"I returned to Memphis with the material you requested."

John paused, thinking, *I'm not going to say another word about Max.*

JOHN WAS ABOUT to leave the convention when he unexpectedly ran into Nicky and Dominic, who had just entered the room. They warmly greeted him and expressed surprise at seeing him, then asked why he was in Lake Tahoe. John informed them that he representing a banking client who was unable to attend, then asked why they were there. Nicky explained that they were working with Max Massey on a project.

John wanted to learn more about their plans, but Nicky saw Max beckoning to him, and he and Dominic abruptly said goodbye. John watched as they walked over to meet Max, but couldn't hear what they were saying. Suddenly Max became very quiet. Nicky was doing the talking and Max was shaking his head up and down like a puppet.

That's exactly what it was! Max was the puppet—and Nicky was the puppet-master pulling the strings. It hit John all at once. Carlos, Nicky and Max were behind this entire venture—because of Nakoma Vista Casino.

GLANCING AT BRENT, Reese quickly voiced, "Suddenly, I had the opportunity to buy property on Lake Tahoe—and I did! My investment has already doubled."

Brent graciously stated, "You surely did see a good thing. I wish I'd been in on that."

"And now, Ms. Janie," Reese smiled, "I'd like to hear all about New Orleans."

Knowing little about Janie's life in the Crescent City, Brent recognized an opportunity. "I'd like to hear, too."

Janie hesitated, carefully centering her response on the evening that she and John had been guests of Nicky and Dominic at Le Saint Clair and her ensuing opportunity to work for April Giovanetti.

DOMINIC ACCOMPANIED JANIE to meet April Giovanetti and assess the remodeling of her house, a nineteenth-century Louisiana-style cottage on La Rue Dauphine. The early morning sun shone brightly as April greeted them outside the small, white-painted wooden gate. She was an attractive blonde with luminous blue eyes, attired in jeans and a petal pink T-shirt. April shook hands with Janie and kissed Dominic. Janie knew at once that April and Dominic were more than casual acquaintances.

Once inside the house, April politely informed Janie, "I want the rooms painted in light colors. I love pink. But, you're the interior decorator; I'll go with whatever you suggest."

Dominic laughed. "Do whatever April wants. Cost is not an issue."

"I'll be glad to do that!" agreed Janie. She thought about each room as she walked through the house, then laid out her plans.

"First, we'll make any necessary repairs. Then we'll paint all of the rooms in delicate shades of pastels to create an airy look. We can stipple the living room and dining room in light blue and install ceiling fans."

Janie continued. "April's bedroom—exactly what she wants: a soft shade of pink, her favorite color."

Dominic frequently stopped by April's to see how work was progressing. He was always accompanied by Nicky, whose interest was Janie, and the foursome would go out together to eat.

After several months, the house began to beautify. In the interim, April and Janie got to know each other and became close friends.

April wanted space to display her keepsakes, and Janie found that the den had adequate wall space to accommodate them. An antique Seth Thomas clock with rich mahogany patina dominated the top shelf of the recessed bookcase.

"This clock," April softly spoke to Janie, "is a family heirloom and I will always cherish it."

The ledge beneath the clock housed a gold-framed portrait of April's parents, Bruno and Donna Giovanetti.

When April's remodel was completed, Dominic and Nicky were both impressed. Dominic then mentioned that he owned a house next door that needed renovation, and asked if Janie would agree to work for them. She was interested.

Nicky offered encouragement. "Go to the Marchesino office and Tina, our receptionist, will take care of the rest. Be sure to tell her I sent you."

After Nicky and Dominic left, April asked Janie to sit. She confided, "Before you take this job, there's something you should know. The house next door is run by a madam. If you don't want to work there because of that, it's alright," April spoke sincerely.

"I still want the job," Janie assured her.

The following morning, Tina was expecting Janie when she arrived at the office of Marchesino Enterprises. Nicky had already informed her of Janie's impending arrival. Tina immediately noted how very attractive this young woman was. This wasn't a routine application; Tina knew that Nicky must have a romantic interest in Janie.

JANIE PAUSED. SHE didn't want her father and Reese to know too much about Nicky.

NICKY WAS A charmer: suave, handsome and mature. Janie adored every moment of Nicky's endless attention. People recognized Nicky and waved at him when they strolled hand in hand through the French Quarter. They enjoyed Creole cuisine—shrimp, crawfish and jambalaya—and spent romantic nights together.

Nicky felt at ease when he was with Janie, sensing that, in some unexplainable way, they understood each other. Like peeling back layers of an onion, Nicky was able to open up and reveal who he was.

Nicky spoke about attending St. Francis Xavier, a Jesuit preparatory school in New Orleans. The other boys knew the Marchesino name and were cautious about getting too friendly.

Dominic Di Paola was also a student at St. Xavier's. Everyone liked Dominic. He quickly realized Nicky's dilemma and tried to get him more socially involved with his classmates.

Dominic and Nicky soon became fast friends; they were always there to support each other.

Nicky told Janie about Father Kevin O'Connor, the chaplain at the school. He was fortyish, short, agile, blue-eyed and redheaded, with a bit of an Irish brogue. All of the students liked Father Kevin because he patiently listened to their problems without passing judgment. He tempered his counseling with understanding.

One day, looking directly at the young man sitting in front of him, Father Kevin asked Nicky, "What do you want to do with your life?" It was a loaded question; the chaplain knew who Nicky's father was. He was attempting to steer Nicky in a different direction.

Father Kevin leaned forward. "Nicky, you're a good person. Someday, you might be tempted to look away from what is right by killing someone, even by your order. That decision would change your life forever."

Father Kevin grasped at the opportunity to further enlighten Nicky. "Your eyes are the windows of your soul as you look at the blue skies, the white clouds and the golden sun. But when you defy the good, that light darkens. You cannot see—you are lost!"

The intensity of Father Kevin's words reflected in his eyes. He hoped to reach Nicky's conscience, and did.

Nicky continued as Janie raptly listened. "Father Kevin had a great influence on my life. He made me think. *Where was I headed? What would I become? What about my father?* Our values were very different."

Nicky hesitated. "I love my father. We talked about this, and he understood. So we decided, for me, only the casinos."

Janie leaned over and hugged Nicky. She realized he was a very complicated individual.

Neither Nicky nor Janie thought about the future that lay before them until reality set in with Teresa, Nicky's wife. Teresa was small in stature and fairly attractive. She highlighted her brown eyes with mascara, and wore a genuine smile that complemented her sunny disposition. Teresa loved Nicky. For the most part, their life together had been fulfilling. The couple had married young and their son, Nicky Jr., brought them abundant joy.

As the years passed, Nicky strayed from the marriage. Then Young Nicky, now twenty-one, announced his decision to become an artist in New York City's Greenwich Village, much to the dismay of both parents.

Teresa was crestfallen about her son leaving home but more despondent knowing that her husband was seeing another woman. Nicky made little effort to conceal his affair. As Teresa became increasingly distraught with Nicky's brazen behavior, she began to put on weight. Her beaming smile disappeared and once-bright eyes revealed hurt and sadness.

After months of unhappiness, Teresa finally turned to Carlos for help. He simply responded, "I'll look into it."

Nicky, summoned to Carlos' office, knew by the Don's solemn expression that the matter was something urgent. Carlos quickly got to the point. "Teresa is worried about you. You've been missing the family dinners. You're never home." Carlos paused to puff on his cigar, then bluntly stated, "You must stop seeing Janie Fox." When Nicky didn't reply, Carlos assumed that the matter was settled.

The following day, Nicky informed Janie about his meeting with his father. He tried to persuade her to continue seeing him, albeit more discreetly. As Janie quietly listened, she realized there would never be any fulfillment in her relationship with Nicky. *I've been so foolish; I must end this affair*, she thought. Nicky was difficult to convince, but Janie was determined. Finally, after a half hour of arguing interspersed with shouting and tears, he reluctantly agreed.

After winning this battle, Janie decided that it would be best to sever all ties with Nicky and the Marchesinos. When she told Nicky that she wanted to quit her job, he was opposed. "I want you to work with Edouard Villon on the Nakoma Vista Casino. Edouard can teach you so much.

"This is an excellent opportunity for you. You said you always wanted your own interior design business. Janie, I want you to have that chance." Nicky's tone was both earnest and commanding.

JANIE NOW ADDRESSED her father, Reese and John, "Nicky wanted me to work at Lake Tahoe, at Nakoma Vista, under Edouard Villon, a well-respected New Orleans contractor. Edouard was a short Cajun man, about sixty, with shaggy gray hair, beady brown eyes and a beaming smile. He was a skilled craftsman—and a demanding perfectionist, too. He called me Mademoiselle Janie.

"Let me tell you about the Nakoma Vista," Janie added. She then described the twelve floors faced with buff-colored adobe, reflective windows and spacious grounds, beautifully landscaped with white-blossomed cactus.

"When the interior was fitted up and ready for decorating, Edouard helped me choose the right colors to brighten the suites and coordinate with the French Provincial furniture." Janie paused, smiling. "He was amazing. I'll always think of him as my mentor."

Reese spoke up. "Lake Tahoe was a big undertaking. Quite a challenge." Then, addressing Brent, "You must be very proud of your daughter."

Brent beamed. "I am."

11

JANIE SMILED DEMURELY at her father. "John is working at Nakoma Vista Casino. He could tell you more."

Brent seemed surprised, and looked at Reese, who replied, "Yes, I knew about that."

Turning to John, Brent adopted an authoritative but friendly tone. "I'd like to hear about this!"

"Mr. Fox," began John, "it all started when you contacted me about Janie. She hadn't called you for a long while and you were worried. You knew that I'd seen her briefly when I went to New Orleans on business. Afterward, I promised you that I'd go back to find out how she was getting along, so I did."

WHEN JOHN ARRIVED in New Orleans, it was warm and sunny. The French Quarter was already bustling. Walking through the narrow, cobblestone streets, John found 875 La Rue Charité, Janie's address. The facade reflected early nineteenth century French Quarter construction, with a heavy, black Tuscan-style wrought iron security gate topped with decorative spears.

John rang the buzzer. When Janie realized who it was, she quickly opened the gate and hugged him, her eyes wide with joyful surprise. Together, they walked through a latticed archway down a moss-covered pathway lined with ferns and flowering ground cover that led to an open red brick courtyard.

John marveled at the character and beauty of what he saw inside: a plethora of pink and white azaleas, blue agapanthus and luxuriant rose oleander, surrounded with six apartments on two floors—three upstairs, three down—all white, accented with dark green shutters and latticed redwood doors.

"There's my apartment," Janie pointed to number one on the first floor. "Come inside and see my place." Shortly, with iced teas in hand, they returned outside and sat on one of several black wrought-iron benches positioned next to a bubbling, stone fountain.

"I can't believe you're here!" Janie smiled.

John explained the reason for his sudden visit.

"It's your father, Janie. He hasn't been able to get in touch with you. He asked me to come and make sure you're okay."

Janie frowned a little. "I should've called him, but I didn't want to tell him about Nicky or where I was living—and that these apartments belong to the Marchesinos. That would have started an argument." Janie emphatically added, "Everyone in New Orleans knows Nicky, and he's fun to be with."

John grasped the picture at once. Janie was attempting to convince him that her life was on track.

"Nicky will be here any minute," smiled Janie. "We're going to the Fair Grounds to see the horse races."

At that moment, the apartment buzzer sounded, and Janie saw Nicky standing at the entrance.

Nicky was outwardly cordial. "Good to see you again, John." However, his thoughts were heavier: *Why is John here? Does he still have an interest in Janie?*

The conversation progressed smoothly when Nicky found out that John was visiting at Janie's father's request. "Would you like to come to the races with Janie and me? We plan on meeting some friends."

John was somewhat reluctant. It was an awkward situation, but Nicky insisted.

When they arrived at the Fair Grounds on Gentilly Boulevard, the racetrack was crowded with people. Many spectators were already seated in the grandstands, poring over their programs. Other bettors preferred to stand near the paddock to see the horses and their brilliantly clad jockeys up close, before making their selections.

Nicky escorted Janie and John to the upper level of the clubhouse, where he was immediately recognized and greeted. They joined Dominic, who was with April in the Marchesino box, overlooking the finish line.

When April was introduced to John, she politely replied, "I'm so glad to meet you." She had heard about John; Janie had discussed him on more than one occasion. Nonetheless, April cautiously refrained from making any remarks that could be misconstrued. She knew about Janie's relationship with Nicky.

April quietly appraised John. She liked him almost immediately. He appeared to be a decent guy, considerate and dependable. John couldn't take his eyes off Janie, who didn't seem to notice; she was too enamored with Nicky.

April had grown up in a Mafia household. She had no choice. But Janie—she wasn't seeing the whole picture.

Janie's face was rosy with excitement as she declared, "I love the races!"

The early contests were fairly predictable. The favorites, with seasoned jockeys astride, crossed the finish line first, yielding small payoffs. Nicky observed that John hadn't bought any tickets but seemed to be enjoying the racing spectacle. Race number seven would begin in ten minutes.

As the thoroughbreds were paraded past the stands on their way to the post, Dominic pointed out a prancing gray horse with its mounted jockey clad in brilliant silks of crimson and royal blue. As they headed toward the starting gate, Dominic leaned over and whispered to Nicky, who called out the name of the horse. "That's Gray Ethel. She's a long shot, but she's going to be an upset—a dark horse," he laughed.

Nicky bought Janie a fifty-dollar win ticket on Gray Ethel, and Dominic bought one for April. "She's ready to go," affirmed Nicky.

He encouraged John, "Take a chance on this horse. Gray Ethel is going to be a winner." Nicky appeared confident, so John, acquiescing to be sociable, purchased a five-dollar ticket. The race was an upset to the favorite, and Gray Ethel—the long shot at forty-to-one—came in the winner, just as Nicky predicted.

Janie and April were overjoyed at their winnings and laughingly taunted John. "You should have bet more!"

John agreed, but added, "I don't like to lose."

Nicky immediately picked up on this remark, asking, "Are you against gambling?"

"Not necessarily," smiled John. "I only gamble on sure things."

Nicky gave Dominic a knowing glance. "John, we might have something that will interest you; but first, I need to talk to my father."

Upon returning to Memphis, John assured Brent, "Janie likes her job and her life in New Orleans. She promised to call you." John purposely mentioned nothing about Nicky.

Several weeks later, John was sitting in his office when he received a telephone call from Nicky. "Can you come to New Orleans? It's a business matter." He didn't elaborate.

John pondered briefly before answering. "Yes."

Nicky then provided instructions. "Alex will have your ticket at LaCrosse Air Charter early Friday morning. Your appointment at our offices will be at two that afternoon."

With a puzzled expression, John slowly replaced the receiver. *What does Nicky Marchesino want with me?*

When John arrived at Marchesino Enterprises, Nicky and Carlos greeted him. Nicky immediately got to the point. "Our reason for approaching you is our new casino, Nakoma Vista in Lake Tahoe. We need an owner until," Nicky paused, "we can quietly take over later. My father and I have talked about it, and we both agree that you would be a good choice." Carlos nodded in assent.

John was silent for a moment, then spoke. "I have a question. I have no experience managing a casino. You could find any number of more qualified businessmen. Why me?"

Carlos now leaned forward, cigar in hand. "Yes, we've considered that, but your stellar reputation in Memphis real estate speaks for itself—*that's the bottom line.*"

"What exactly would I be doing?" John quickly asked.

Nicky asserted, "Your main objective would be to get the casino license, which has to be granted by the Nevada Gaming Control Board. It can't have any connection with Marchesino Enterprises. You would be listed as owner on the application."

Glancing at his father, Nicky continued, "Edouard Villon is our contractor. Construction is underway, but Edouard hates paperwork. You would be the manager in charge of subcontractors, purchasing supplies, paying invoices, payroll—everything to keep this project moving.

"Moreover," added Nicky, "you've met Dominic. He'll be running Nakoma Vista when the work's completed, and he's fully qualified to manage a casino."

Nicky asked his father to explain further. Carlos was quite specific. "You might have to be in Lake Tahoe for a year or more." He promptly proposed a hefty figure. "I hope this would compensate you for your change of venue. Is this agreeable?"

Carlos and Nicky quietly waited for John's reply. The offer was tempting but John was reticent, remembering Max Massey, who had once been connected with Nakoma Vista Casino. *Where was he?*

Nicky, immediately aware of John's hesitation, quickly interjected in a smooth voice, "I meant to tell you; Janie Fox is now working in Lake Tahoe." John's eyes widened.

Nicky knew that he had captured John's attention. "I thought you might enjoy working with Janie. She'll be there for quite some time."

John's decision was made. He calmly responded, "I'll take the job."

Nicky and Carlos looked pleased.

JOHN TURNED DIRECTLY to Brent. "I had a good reason to go to Lake Tahoe. I was offered a very lucrative position." He chose not to elaborate further.

Janie quickly interrupted. "I was surprised to see John at Nakoma Vista. I had no idea that he would be working there. We were both busy all day, but our nights were so quiet and peaceful.

"We stayed in a two-story, rustic lodge on the Lake Tahoe property, surrounded by Ponderosa pines. John, Edouard and I each had a furnished suite. Edouard was an excellent chef, and on evenings when it was warm enough, we'd sit on the deck, eating steaks or freshly caught trout—grilled to perfection."

"Actually," John added, "everything seemed to come together with Dominic's arrival and installation of the gaming equipment."

OPENING DAY AT Nakoma Vista Casino was approaching. Nicky had flown in from New Orleans and was impressed.

The casino's debut was a notable event. Crowds of people gathered to see Lake Tahoe's newest palatial gambling house. John, as owner, was highly visible, with Janie at his side for the ribbon-cutting.

That evening, the banquet room was elegantly decorated for guests invited to the grandiose affair. John was seated at the head table with Edouard and Janie. The mayor of Lake Tahoe presided; numerous politicians and a sprinkling of celebrities and athletes attended. The news media generated pre-opening publicity for the casino and provided coverage of the event.

As guests were finishing dessert, the mayor addressed the guests. He then presented Certificates of Appreciation from the City of Lake Tahoe to each of the honorees: John and Edouard. John noticed Nicky quietly standing in the rear doorway of the banquet hall. Photographers with flashing cameras were focused on a radiant Janie, as Edouard presented her with a gold-framed award for artistic design. Nicky had personally arranged this recognition for Janie. Culminating more than a year of hard work, the opening ceremonies were a memorable occasion.

On her last evening at Lake Tahoe before leaving for New Orleans, Janie sat with John on the porch of their rustic lodge. Relaxing contentedly, Janie rested her head on John's shoulder as they viewed Nakoma Vista, with completion ending their work together.

Janie suddenly spoke. "I'm glad I came to Tahoe. Monsieur Villon inspired me to do my best. I really liked him and enjoyed working with him."

Gently, she added, "John, what brought you here? I keep wondering."

There was a quiet moment as John reflected. *What should I say?* Finally, "Only one reason, Janie. I came to be with you."

JANIE NOW ADDRESSED her father and Reese. "I rode with Nicky to the Lake Tahoe airport. He suggested that I open my own interior design business in the French Quarter. Nicky had talked to April Giovanetti, who was willing to rent me office space in her Louisiana cottage and put a sign in her yard."

Brent quickly asked, "Who is this April? What does she do?"

Before Janie could reply, Eva Fox appeared. "Our guests are starting to arrive, Brent. This is *your* party! Come and say hello."

As they all left the den, Janie looked up at John and softly whispered, "Thank you."

While Brent Fox and William Reese cordially mingled with their business acquaintances, Eva proudly presented Janie to her friends. Many of them hadn't seen Janie for years.

The guests enjoyed hors d'oeuvres served on linen-covered silver trays—jumbo shrimp, crostini, bruschetta and antipasto—followed by a sumptuous buffet that included meat, seafood and vegetarian dishes. After refreshing their drinks, John and Janie leisurely walked out to the garden, bedecked with colorful Japanese hanging paper lanterns to illuminate the way.

They were sitting at a small, white wrought-iron table with a vase of forget-me-nots, quietly smoking their cigarettes when John broke the silence. "Janie, there's something you need to know. It's about the FBI, and it happened after you left Lake Tahoe."

SEVERAL WEEKS AFTER Nakoma Vista's grand opening, John sat at his office desk reviewing the proceeds, which confirmed that the casino was performing well. His secretary, working at her desk in the outer office, was startled when two FBI agents suddenly walked in and demanded to see John Harrison. Without announcing their arrival, she quickly ushered the men into his office.

When they presented their credentials, the names—Dale Russell and Brad Barnett—hit John. *I know them both. They're older now, but they're the same FBI agents that I met at Big Bob's.*

Agent Russell chose to acknowledge no recognition and calmly spoke. "We're here to ask you if you know Max Massey. He was presumed to be the former owner of Nakoma Vista Casino."

Russell paused. "Max was last seen leaving Lake Tahoe for New Orleans. Are you aware that he's missing?"

Though the word "missing" stunned John, he maintained his composure. *Now I know what happened to Max!*

Side-stepping Russell's direct question, John replied firmly, "I only saw Max Massey once—at an investment meeting in Lake Tahoe. That was a few years ago."

Russell wasn't deterred by John's evasive answer. "We're sure that Max Massey went to see Carlos Marchesino," he added in a serious tone, "no doubt about Nakoma Vista Casino."

John remained silent when Russell announced, "I have something to show you."

He opened his black leather briefcase, removed a folder containing a photograph of three people and placed it before John. Russell first pointed to Max Massey. "These two with

Max are Gino Marchesino and Dominic Di Paola. Our agents took this picture at Romano's Restaurant."

Russell looked at Barnett, then stressed to John, "That's the last time Max Massey was ever seen."

Expressionless, John eyed Russell and responded firmly, "Like I said, I only saw Max once. I can't help you."

Russell was not pleased.

Barnett stepped forward. "John, I have something to show you."

He took out another photograph. "This one was taken at LaCrosse's Lake Tahoe airport—Nicky Marchesino and Janie Fox. We know Nicky is connected to Nakoma Vista which," Barnett added sarcastically, "is a shell corporation for Marchesino Enterprises."

Russell now spoke. "We'll find out what happened to Max," he paused, "and when we do, you'll most likely lose your casino."

John suddenly stood and motioned toward the door. "I think you need to go."

Russell and Barnett briskly walked out.

IN THE FOX'S garden, Janie was pensive, carefully weighing what John had just disclosed.

"I never knew Max Massey, but now I understand why you have that job."

John nodded. "And now Nicky wants me to stay on longer before I leave Nakoma Vista. That's not what I had in mind."

Just then, Eva Fox appeared on the patio, waving for everyone to come inside for the main event.

The dining room was elaborately set for the gala gathering. First, a champagne toast; then a strawberry-filled cake with white frosting, decorated with the name *Fox Brokerage* in red letters and lighted with tiny candles. Brent stood in the midst of his well-wishers; most importantly, his wife and daughter. It was a euphoric moment for him.

John, standing nearby, sensed in Brent something else: his regret for interfering in Janie's life. Had that not happened, Janie would never have met the Marchesinos.

12

THE EARLY SUNDAY morning sun rose over the River Bluff condominium, providing a brief but tranquil respite. John gazed at Janie with tenderness. He realized that so much in their lives had changed, but his hopes for a renewed relationship brightened.

That afternoon, Janie and John walked with Sharon and Chris to W.C. Handy Park on Beale Street. As a crowd started to gather, couples were strolling together in the warm sun.

Tyrone was standing near Handy's statue when he spotted his friends and rushed over to greet them.

"I'm so glad you're here!" Tyrone's face was animated as he eagerly shook hands.

"Couldn't miss coming!" responded John with a grin. "We remember all your great songs."

"That goes back to when we first became friends." Tyrone added, "Remember how we used to hang out at the Keystone Drive-in?" He smiled. "Everyone went from car to car to say hello, then y'all would come over and join me and my pals, sitting on the low concrete block wall. That was 1969—things were a lot different then. I'd play my guitar and we'd all be having a good time until Ernie the bully showed up."

"I can't forget Ernie," continued Tyrone, "He didn't like me. John, I'll always remember how you stood up to him for me."

ERNIE HAD MENACING dark eyes, brown hair slicked with pomade and combed straight back, and a grin that didn't necessarily mean he liked you—those were his trademarks. He enjoyed heckling. His intimidation and muscular, solid build sent many an adversary on his way.

Ernie was full of himself, wearing his faded, baggy blue jeans, gray T-shirt and leather jacket. He puffed on his cigarette and flicked it in John and Tyrone's direction, contemptuously yelling, "You shouldn't be over there."

What he really meant was that John shouldn't be sitting with Tyrone. But John didn't let Ernie get away with that. He stood up and shouted back, "Tyrone's my friend. I'll sit with him if I want to." Ernie, angry that anyone would dare to confront him in front of his peers, challenged John to fight him after school the following Monday.

The infamous day arrived. By three-fifteen, most students were leaving the school grounds, except those headed toward the large heating plant located behind the school. They knew that this was the place to see a fight.

When the students arrived, Ernie was already strutting confidently before his supporters. Most onlookers thought that John was sure to lose the fight. Suddenly, two unexpected figures emerged from the thoroughfare. There were whispers among the small crowd as the strangers approached. Someone said, "That's Joey Bellisario and Big Bob!" There was no mistaking them; they were familiar figures at the neighborhood bowling alley.

Joey slowly walked up to John, with Big Bob next to him. Joey turned and stepped in Ernie's direction, speaking clearly. "John told me about your fight and now that I'm here," Joey paused, aware that the crowd was hanging onto his every word, "I can see that this won't be a fair one. Ernie, you're much bigger—you outweigh John. I think we're about the same size, though. How about I fight you in John's place?" Joey's voice had a sharp edge. Big Bob nodded in agreement, puffing his cigar.

There was a dead silence in the crowd. Everyone was waiting for Ernie to answer.

Joey's words were like a thunderbolt. Ernie looked stunned. His face paled and eyes widened. He knew trouble when he saw it, and Joey Bellisario was *major* trouble.

TYRONE SMILED AT Janie and Sharon. "Ernie didn't really have much of a choice. To save face, he agreed that it wouldn't be a fair fight and said he would call it off—if John was willing. John agreed, but everyone could tell that Ernie was just trying to hide the fact that he was scared of Joey."

Tyrone laughed. "The Keystone parking lot was much better after that confrontation! Ernie and his buddies never bothered any of us again."

The musical performance that Tyrone had arranged in W. C. Handy Park was well received and accompanied by bursts of applause and loud whistling.

Tyrone was enthusiastic about prospects for Beale Street's future. He asked Chris, "Do you want to be a part of the committee?"

Chris advised him, "I'm afraid we can't do that."

"Why not?" questioned Tyrone with a puzzled look.

Chris was hesitant, but John spoke up. "Tyrone, we've had recent business dealings with people in New Orleans about Beale Street. There may be a conflict of interest."

Tyrone's eyes opened wide. Nothing slipped past him. He was aware of The Big One in New Orleans and already knew that John had connections there.

Tyrone simply acknowledged, "I understand."

Chris hurriedly interjected, "But we can contribute!"

"That'll be appreciated," replied Tyrone.

After the concert, the four friends, happy and lighthearted, were walking back to River Bluff Condominiums when they spotted Brent Fox, William Reese and Captain Spencer walking a short distance ahead.

"Let's catch up and say hello," suggested Janie.

Chris and Sharon agreed; John was reluctant. Something was up.

They all met in front of Reese's condominium, but Reese, aware that Captain Spencer was agitated, politely excused himself. Spencer suddenly pulled John and Chris aside.

Charles Spencer imposed a commanding figure. John was apprehensive—and quickly discovered why. Spencer addressed him in an accusing voice. "John, we know that your job at the Nakoma Vista Casino is a cover-up for the Marchesinos."

Captain Spencer held a stern expression, his eyes gravely focused on John. "I've warned you before but," he threw up his hands, "you're making decisions that aren't just wrong—they're dangerous!"

Still disturbed, the captain turned to Chris. "And you—*my own son*—taking on a client like Paul Alfonso, who owns all the strip clubs in Memphis! I realize, with your law practice, you have to make certain choices, but this is one client you should have turned away. It disappoints me to see *either* of you involved with the Marchesinos. You both need to reevaluate your priorities."

Spencer's contorted expression of disapproval underscored his disgust. Chris remained silent, trying to ignore John's surprise; he knew nothing about Chris' business with Paul Alfonso.

Captain Spencer bluntly announced, "Everyone please go. Mr. Fox and I have a private matter to discuss with his daughter."

From the patio of Chris' condominium, John's eyes were transfixed on the three figures still standing on the walkway: Janie, her father and Captain Spencer. John couldn't hear what they were saying but closely observed their body language. Janie listened intently to an animated Captain Spencer as her father silently watched.

Eight minutes later, a brow-beaten Janie arrived and sat down on the sofa to join her friends.

John asked, "Are you all right?"

"I'm fine," Janie replied with a flushed face and distressed voice. Her carefree spirit, so evident earlier, had disappeared. Janie paused. Displaying an anxious look, she nervously lit a cigarette. "Something came up about my business in April's house in the French Quarter."

THE OFFICE FOR Interior Designs, Janie's business, was a sunroom adjacent to the living room of April Giovanetti's house, suitable for the ambience and privacy that her clients needed. The large rectangular room was furnished with a mahogany desk, straight-back mahogany chairs and long wooden table to display catalogues containing samples of vibrant materials.

This particular day had been busy, with a serious client poring over colorful designs to make her final decision. Janie felt good about this. She enjoyed completing the sale.

It was nearly five o'clock, time to leave the office. Janie walked to the door of the study to wave goodbye to April, who motioned for her to come in and meet Dawn. Dawn was a stunningly attractive young woman with intriguing green eyes and flowing, wavy chestnut brown hair.

She greeted Janie warmly. "I live in the house next door that you redecorated. You do great work."

Janie, pleased by Dawn's compliment, graciously answered, "Thank you."

Preparing to leave, Dawn rose from her chair and handed a large white envelope to April. She immediately placed it in her desk drawer.

After Dawn left, April hesitated, then said, "Janie, there's something I should have told you when you started renting here. But first, I have a special Tuscan liqueur, a Galliano. Would you like to try it with me?" Janie nodded.

"This is very nice," she smiled as they sipped the golden ambrosia.

Speaking softly, April revealed, "I manage an escort service."

She noted Janie's astounded expression. "Don't look so shocked. Sex is always somewhere on the scene. Why not carefully arranged evening dates?"

She anxiously awaited Janie's response.

"How did you get into that?" Janie asked.

April slowly began. "When I was eighteen, my life changed when my mother died. My father, Bruno, worked at The Bourbon Burlesque. I wanted to be independent, but my choices were limited with the Giovanetti name, so my father gave me a job bartending at his club.

"I learned a lot—people, sex, drugs. Then something wonderful happened." April's face lit up. "Dominic Di Paola came to the club on business. He would often stop at the bar to talk to me and I fell in love with him, Janie. He cared about me—he loved me."

April added, "Dominic didn't want me to work at the Bourbon Burlesque anymore, so we came up with the idea to start an upscale escort service.

"We always carefully screened our escorts so we could attract sophisticated, discreet evening dates for our clientele—which includes wealthy men and politicians. We charge an appropriate fee. It wasn't long before I was able to buy this house."

April paused, waiting for Janie to comment.

"April," Janie slowly spoke in a consoling voice, "if I had been in your place, maybe I would have done what you did. I understand."

With a radiant smile, April raised her cordial stem. "To you and me!"

THERE WAS A sudden silence in Chris' condominium. John walked out alone to the patio to reflect on what he'd just heard about April's escort service and Janie's business in her house. *What can I say to Janie? April is her friend.*

Glancing up, John saw Janie holding a Heineken and smiling. "Thought you might like this. I'm surprised you didn't have something to say to me about April."

John's eyes held an inquisitive look. "Would you have listened? Since you mentioned it, I'll say this now, Janie. *Be careful!*"

Janie responded with a determined tone, "John, I'm going to talk to my father about the scene that he and Captain Spencer made on the Riverbluff Walkway. Several people noticed—it was demeaning—and embarrassing!"

The next morning, Janie drove John's Cadillac slowly up the long driveway of the Fox home.

Brent was sitting in the den, sportily attired, watching the Wimbledon matches on their large television console. He was pleasantly surprised to see his daughter.

"I'm so glad you're here! Your mother's over at the country club, but she'll be back in a little while. Sit down and watch the tennis match with me—Jimmy Connors is winning."

Janie didn't comply. She walked over to the television, turned it off and stood defiantly before her father. Brent realized that she was furious.

Janie spoke out rudely, "You told Captain Spencer that my new business in New Orleans is in April Giovanetti's house—and you questioned her integrity! You didn't respect what I told you in confidence."

Brent was startled. He hadn't expected this outburst from Janie but knew he had to justify his reason for asking Captain Spencer to speak with her.

"Charles Spencer is a longtime family friend and he knows how concerned I am for you. As captain of the Organized Crime Unit, he has access to confidential information. I'm sure you know that April's father is Bruno Giovanetti, a Mafia club owner." Brent paused with an anxious expression.

"Janie, I don't know April and I'm not going to pass judgment about her personally, but she runs an escort service from her house. The FBI will come after her! When they do, where does that leave you?" Brent was determined to convince Janie.

She flatly declared, "I only rent office space for my work."

Brent sighed heavily. "Janie, you might still be caught up in all of this." He suddenly stood, reached out and hugged her. "Why don't you come back to Memphis? I'll help you find a place for your interior design business here."

Janie's face softened. "I can't do that right now—perhaps later. I appreciate your offer, though." She cracked a small smile. "I do love you, Dad, but you have to let me be my own person."

13

JOHN'S MEMPHIS VISIT was drawing to an end. John, with Janie beside him, reflected as he drove to Alex LaCrosse's Air Charter, *How quickly time passed during that brief, unforgettable weekend.*

When John and Janie entered the waiting room, Philippa hailed John. "I don't have a ticket for you. When did you call?"

"I'm not flying today, Philippa," John explained. "Just Janie Fox."

Philippa recognized Janie and knew that both she and John worked in Lake Tahoe. Until now, she hadn't seen the couple together. Philippa sensed an intimacy between them as John gently hugged Janie and kissed her goodbye.

Philippa was aware that Nicky always arranged Janie's airplane tickets. Although she was curious, she knew when not to ask questions—and this was definitely such a time.

All of the waiting passengers were soon alerted to board the plane for New Orleans.

John thought as he slowly walked back to his car, *Janie casually mentioned coming back to Memphis, but not right away. By the time she's ready, I should be able to leave Nakoma Vista.*

Two FBI agents sat in an unmarked Chevrolet Nova parked on an incline, several hundred feet away from Alex's property in the government parking lot at the Federal Aviation Administration's offices, near the airport's control tower. They had been assigned to surveillance at LaCrosse Air Charter to monitor the money being flown to the Marchesinos.

The senior FBI agent, about fifty, slightly gray and neatly attired, had already spotted John through his binoculars.

The younger agent, in his thirties and proficient at using a telescopic camera, had earlier photographed John and Janie entering the LaCrosse building.

"Well," commented the older agent, "John Harrison just got into his car—alone. Janie Fox must be flying back to New Orleans. We know who they're working for." He shook his head. "Might take some time—but we'll get both of them."

LaCrosse's plane took off and Janie settled back in her seat, mulling over her father's offer of assistance. She had assured him that having her office at April's house wasn't a problem. Then she suddenly recalled that late afternoon in April's den—Dawn and the envelope she'd given to April. At that time, it hadn't seemed important, but now Janie was reflecting. *Could the envelope have contained money? My father might be right! Maybe it's best that I don't know.*

John joined Chris in his Rawlins House office as they both enjoyed their morning coffee ritual. John was the first to mention Paul Alfonso.

"Chris, I want to hear all about your new client. How did you get roped into being Paul's lawyer?"

Chris paused with an embarrassed look. "I should have told you sooner, John. Joey Bellisario and Paul Alfonso came to see me about a month ago. Joey remembered me from the couple of times I came with you to Big Bob's. Paul explained that he had some strip clubs and adult movie theaters, and needed to be sure that he was properly licensed."

Chris paused. "Joey knows that my father is Captain Spencer with the OCU. He probably expects that having me as his lawyer will help him if there's any trouble. I did hesitate at first, but they offered me a hefty retainer for my legal work, and Alfonso's licensing requirements were just a business matter."

John was half smiling. "I can almost guarantee you, Chris; they're going to want more. I made a huge mistake when I agreed to allow Janie to meet Nicky Marchesino. Janie's been my biggest worry," John paused, "and now you're involved, too."

Upon returning to New Orleans, Janie arrived at Marchesino Enterprises, accompanied by April. April had convinced Janie that she should inform Nicky about Captain Spencer. Tina greeted both young women with a warm smile. The receptionist was aware that Carlos wasn't pleased with Nicky's interest in Janie. However, Tina also knew that Carlos had left for the day.

"I'll take you to Nicky's office," Tina said, leading the way as her footsteps echoed in the hallway. "It's almost five o'clock and I'm about to leave."

Nicky's office was well appointed with an expensive, Italian Modern executive office set. The ambience was formal, yet comfortable.

When Janie and April were both seated, an oil portrait hanging directly behind Nicky's desk caught Janie's attention. She knew that Nicky Jr. had painted this scene: a wizened Cajun fisherman sitting in his pirogue, fishing pole in hand. Nicky was exceptionally proud of his son's painting.

Nicky regarded Janie with dark, questioning eyes. Although their relationship had ended, he still harbored deep feelings for her.

Nicky casually asked, "How was your father's retirement party?" He knew of the event.

With a cheery smile, Janie assured him, "The party was fabulous and the weekend was enjoyable, for the most part." She suddenly paused, and Nicky immediately sensed that her mood had changed.

He then glanced at April, who was unusually quiet.

Janie explained to Nicky, "My father is concerned about me running my business from April's house. He told his friend, Captain Charles Spencer, who oversees Memphis' Organized Crime Unit. They're determined to run the Marchesinos out of Memphis. That means they're after Carlos, your father!"

Garnering a serious expression, Nicky assured her. "Janie, I'll investigate this problem. I know Captain Spencer has no love for the Marchesinos, and neither does your father."

He smiled. "I'll find somewhere else for your office. Maybe April's house isn't the best place." Nicky presumed that the matter was settled.

April quickly interjected, "I already suggested that. I explained to Janie that if she needs to leave, I'll understand."

Janie stared directly at Nicky. "You arranged for me to have my office in April's house—and the sign in her yard has already attracted clients. I really don't intend to move!"

Nicky, fully aware that Janie was a firebrand, prudently replied, "If you change your mind, just tell me, and we'll find you a new place."

"I feel so relieved," Janie confided to April after they left Nicky's office. "I really appreciate you coming with me."

"It was something you had to do," agreed April.

Nicky sat quietly in his high-back, leather office chair. He couldn't deny that seeing Janie again had aroused suppressed emotions. Janie looked as charming as ever, graced with her Southern gentility and cultured manners. He even remembered her flawless French when she had ordered her entree that first evening they met.

Nicky pondered, *In spite of everything, perhaps Janie is still concerned about me and Carlos.*

That evening, Nicky drove his black limousine into the grand entrance of the Marchesino estate in Mandeville, draped with willow trees and flowering gardenia bushes. Their family home was a spacious two-story, buff brick French Provincial manor.

Set off to the right was Nicky and Teresa's white bungalow, with its French windows opening onto a garden of gorgeous red and pink roses that exuded a mystifying fragrance.

Carlos didn't need an army of guards to patrol the premises; he treasured uninterrupted quietude and serenity—and staunchly defended his turf. Mafia crime bosses and their families understood that Louisiana was strictly off limits—except by his invitation.

Angela Marchesino, Nicky's mother, greeted her son warmly, as she accompanied him, Teresa and Carlos into the formal dining room of the stately mansion for a family dinner. She was attractively gowned in a pale blue, silk dress that revealed a slender figure.

At sixty-one, Angela still reflected the Sicilian beauty that had attracted Carlos years ago. Her smartly-styled, lustrous black hair showed only a trace of silver. With penetrating brown eyes, her flawless complexion revealed a few fine lines. Angela's face and brown eyes radiated an elegant beauty. She had spent her adult life as the matriarch of a Mafia family. Carlos loved and respected Angela.

Nicky's wife was at his side. Teresa's eyes gleamed with happiness—Nicky was home. She was elated that his affair with Janie Fox had ended.

Angela gaily announced, "It's your favorite dinner, Nicky! Veal parmigiana, pasta primavera, Caesar salad, and of course," she smiled, "your father's special wine, a Marsala."

Carlos took his seat at the head of the table in a dignified manner. Family dinners were always a special occasion. Nonetheless, he noticed that Nicky conveyed a serious and urgent look, indicating that they must talk later.

At eight-thirty, Nicky and Carlos retired to the den for an after-dinner brandy.

The den was Carlos' retreat. There, he could relax in his easy chair with his humidor, stocked with his favorite El Producto cigars, close at hand. The room was masculine, with dark mahogany paneling and hardwood floors partially covered by an oriental rug. Burgundy draperies accentuated the elongated casement windows. An oversized painting of the Roman Coliseum, replete with gladiators, slaves and spectators, hung on the wall. Its artist had brilliantly captured the intense combat.

A white marble bust of the first Roman emperor, Caesar Augustus, was mounted atop a darkened teakwood stand, prominently displayed in one corner of the room.

Roman culture fascinated Carlos. Though he had little formal schooling, he sought to learn everything about the history of his ancestors.

Nicky quickly updated his father about Janie's message. "It seems," Nicky added, "we have a problem."

Carlos drew heavily on his cigar. "I regret that this matter has drawn Spencer's interest. I don't want to attract attention in Memphis. Gino oversees everything we do there. Maybe if I tell you about Gino and me, you'll better understand who we are."

Carlos paused to drop the ash from his cigar into a large ceramic ashtray. His eyes focused intensely on Nicky. "Gino and I had a good life in Sicily. Our family was well off until the late Thirties. Then Mussolini and his Blackshirts started arresting men who weren't members of the Fascist party. Mafia men were singled out and killed. Our father was among them.

"Gino and I were only in our twenties, and we knew we had to find a way to get out. We had friends who arranged our passage out of Sicily. We arrived in the United States and eventually made our way to New Orleans.

"Cargo ships were constantly docking at the Port of New Orleans so we found jobs as longshoremen there. They paid us stevedore's wages—about five dollars a day." Carlos paused.

"Gino was always bold and he got caught stealing. We were both fired immediately. Gino was so angry that he waylaid our boss later that night and beat him badly.

"The police captured Gino and he was sent to prison. The guards were sadistic and most of the inmates hated foreigners. It was a humiliating, terrifying experience for Gino. He vowed that no one would ever send him back to prison.

"Gino and I lived in a tough New Orleans neighborhood, so we had to band together for our own safety. That's how we became the Marchesino Family. We fought together against the odds, even though we didn't always agree. I liked to think first—Gino took immediate action."

Angela suddenly appeared in the doorway of the study. "May I come in?" she asked. As both nodded in assent, she entered.

"It's past the hour, Carlos. You have to take your medicine," she insisted. Donning a bright visage to hide her concern, Angela gave her husband two small pills. Noticing the cigar, she simply said, "You shouldn't," as she left the room.

Carlos, regarding a silent Nicky, continued. "We were talking about Gino and me, and there *is* something I need to discuss with you. I once promised that I wouldn't ask you to take my place as Don. But," Carlos looked pointedly at Nicky, "that means that Gino is next in line. I want you to think about that."

14

TWO FBI AGENTS sat in their car parked in the FAA lot near LaCrosse Air Charter, drinking coffee from Styrofoam cups and scanning the starry sky. One commented, "A beautiful full moon; silvery blue. But look—there it is!" He now pointed toward a white Cessna Citation as it approached the landing strip.

For several weeks, these FBI agents had been monitoring Lou Marchesino's departures and returns from New Orleans.

"Right on time," said the agent with the telescopic camera, photographing Lou carrying a brown leather attaché case and getting into Captain Patrick Lafferty's squad car.

At this point, Lafferty and Lou pulled away. The FBI followed.

Shortly, the FBI agents were parked at a popular Mexican restaurant on Summer Avenue, across from Lili's Cabaret.

They watched as Captain Lafferty dropped Lou at the front door of Paul Alfonso's club, then parked a little further down to wait in his car. Lou opened the opaque oval-shaped black glass door to enter the nightclub's lobby.

Several photographs of featured entertainers were mounted on dark maroon walls. One of the club's girls seated at a small table collected cover charges from two customers. When she saw Lou, she waved him through the doors. Flashing, multi-colored strobe lights surrounded the stage area and performing stripper. Patrons seated at tables were ogling the dancers.

David Coradini, Paul's assistant manager, spotted Lou and immediately greeted him. He was familiar with Lou's visits.

Lou readily recognized that the club's clientele was freely spending, as dollar bills and larger denominations floated around the stage area. As alcoholic beverages were endlessly served, exotic dancers could be seen at several tables performing lap dances for customers. This generated substantial revenue for both the girls and the house.

Lou noticed cocaine and no particular attempt to conceal its use. It had become an increasingly popular drug. Lili's was a huge cash generator, as were Alfonso's other clubs.

Paul was seated at a table enjoying a highball with the attractive hostess, a ravishing redhead with heavy makeup, who was wearing a brocaded bra, silver lame tights and silver stiletto-heeled pumps. Paul rose to greet Lou and instructed David to bring Lou whatever he wanted to drink. Lou declined; his usual reply. He was at Paul's for business, not pleasure.

Paul immediately dismissed the girl. "I'll see you later, Toots." David also turned to leave, and Lou accompanied Paul to his office.

The two FBI agents at the Mexican restaurant were waiting when Lou left the club. "There he is!" exclaimed the younger agent, taking several photographs of Lou with his leather briefcase as he got into Lafferty's car.

"Gotta be the money for the Lili's Cabarets. I'll bet they're going to Big Bob's next," voiced the older agent, as they started the engine and began to follow.

Shortly, they were parked in front of Big Bob's, watching Lou and Lafferty go inside and come out soon after.

The younger agent immediately snapped more photographs of Lou and Lafferty. "That leather briefcase—has to be gambling and bookmaking money! You can bet they're headed for the airport."

The two FBI agents then returned to the FAA parking lot. The older agent called Dale Russell from his car radio. "Lou Marchesino is at LaCrosse Air Charter. Are there any orders?"

Agent Russell responded, "Just a minute." He made a call to the FAA to obtain a list of passengers.

After several minutes, Russell responded. "Lou Marchesino is flying to New Orleans, but *not* Alex, so we're going to hold off for now."

In the conference room of Marchesino Enterprises in New Orleans, Carlos was seated at the head of a long solid African mahogany table inlaid with the Marchesino family crest. Carlos was visibly disturbed. He had called a meeting with consigliere Henri Le Beau and Gino regarding matters in Memphis.

Carlos and Henri drank espresso while they waited for Gino. Neither was conducive to small talk, given the gravity of the situation.

Henri seized this opportunity to counsel his client. "Carlos, Gino is in charge of Alfonso's cabarets. You surely realize that sex clubs also cater to the drug trade—and that's where you're going to run into problems. I'm trying to look out for you." Henri's expression grew intense. "Remember Lucky Luciano? That's what got *him* in trouble."

Before Henri could say more, Gino arrived and quickly handed Carlos the money bag from Memphis.

Carlos immediately informed him of the critical situation with Alfonso's strip clubs. "I'm worried, Gino. Your son, Lou, represents your business interests there. He could get caught up in this."

Henri nodded in agreement.

Carlos added, "Make sure there are no more drugs."

Gino looked surprised but simply replied, "I'll inform Lou."

Gino returned to his residence in Old Metairie. The comfortable interior of his graystone Italianate manor home featured elegant decor. Gino's wife, Louisa, kept a low profile; her life completely centered around her home and family.

It was late afternoon on a hot Tuesday, and Lou was immersed in the family's backyard pool while his girlfriend, the buxom blonde, relaxed on an inflatable raft. Looking up, Lou saw his father standing on the sunny deck beckoning to him. Lou emerged from the water and threw a plush towel around his broad shoulders as he plopped down on one of the deck chairs. Gino poured a glass of iced tea and addressed his son. "Carlos says no more drugs—it's too much of a risk."

Lou stopped short, with anger glaring in his dark eyes. "I don't like this. Carlos can't stop the drugs. If he does, other dealers are going to take over the strip clubs and the prostitution business. We'll lose all that money!" Lou spoke emphatically, "Carlos and Nicky are only interested in the casinos. Carlos must be getting old."

Gino was quietly thinking, *That's true; Carlos is beginning to show his age*. Gino already fancied himself as the next Don.

At Lili's Cabaret on Summer Avenue, Paul asked David to step into his office.

"Is there a problem?" David inquired.

"Yeah, there is," voiced Paul. "I just got a call from Lou. We won't be getting any more cocaine."

"How come?" David asked.

Paul was abrupt. "Lou said that order came from the top. He didn't tell me why. We still have a sizeable stash we need to get rid of."

"That won't be a problem," answered David.

"Maybe that's a good thing," Paul added thoughtfully. "Then we won't have to worry about something going wrong."

Captain Charles Spencer was awakened by the sound of knocking at the back door of his home in High Point Terrace. The red brick house was quiet and dark. On the nightstand, a small digital clock displayed the time: *3:28 AM*.

Spencer rose quickly, turned on the light, grabbed his navy blue, flannel bathrobe and hurried to the kitchen. Looking out, he saw a familiar face and immediately opened the door.

Shortly, they were seated at the small kitchen table with steaming cups of coffee. Captain Spencer was intently listening to his young friend and protégé.

The captain reflected on how it all began.

CAPTAIN SPENCER HAD been asked to teach a course on criminology at Memphis State University. David Coradini, a senior, attended his class. Captain Spencer recognized that this young man was an outstanding student, displaying enthusiasm and constantly asking questions about police work. David was athletic, well-disciplined and street-savvy. His aspirations and handsomely dark Italian features were conducive to undercover work. However, David's driving motive was a desire to restore dignity to his Italian heritage and name.

Upon graduation, David submitted his application to the Organized Crime Unit with Captain Spencer's recommendation. He was accepted and immediately sent out of town for special training, a measure implemented to conceal his identity and employment.

Captain Spencer fortuitously recognized the break they needed for an undercover agent.

A new Lili's Cabaret located between Memphis International Airport and Elvis Presley's Graceland was scheduled to open soon. David Coradini approached Paul Alfonso at Lili's on Summer Avenue and politely introduced himself. "I heard about the new club opening in Whitehaven, not far from Graceland, and I'd like to work there—if you'll give me a chance. I really need a job," he added earnestly.

Paul, surprised by this young man's bold move, questioned, "How did you know about me? Have you ever been here before?"

"I've only been here once with some friends—but," David added, smiling warmly, "everyone knows who you are."

Paul was visibly impressed. He liked what he saw: a clean-cut, young fellow, tall, personable and casually but neatly attired. Most importantly, he had an Italian name, Coradini, which Paul recognized as a reputable family.

He replied with a friendly nod, "We might have something for you. Check back with me in a few days. I'll let you know then."

After David left, Paul began to consider his options. His current manager was experienced and well-rounded—a perfect fit for his new Whitehaven club. Paul thought, *If I hire this young man here at Lili's, I can teach him everything he needs to know.*

Paul smiled to himself. He had already made his decision.

DAVID, SEATED COMFORTABLY in the kitchen with Captain Spencer, suddenly put down his coffee cup, took a small microcassette out of his boot and handed it to his superior. "Lou's deliveries to Lili's Cabaret are going to stop. The order came from New Orleans."

Captain Spencer nodded. "This changes our game plan." He paused. "Now let's talk about what we *do* have."

"When Lou arrived," David said, "he'd go with Paul to his office. I never actually saw Lou give the cocaine to Paul. Then Lou would head out the front door. After that, I'd handle the drugs for the dancers and the money for Paul. Lou would always return the following week with a new shipment and collect."

Captain Spencer looked thoughtful. "There's enough to nail Paul, but not Lou."

David responded disappointedly. "I was hoping we could get Lou. He's behind this entire setup. What can we do?"

"Maybe we still can," said Spencer, breaking a smile.

"Aha!" uttered David. "*Now* I gotcha."

When Lou arrived at Lili's Cabaret the following week, David was standing near the front entrance.

"I'll take you to Paul," announced David. "He's at one of the tables. He knew you were coming."

As soon as Paul saw Lou, they entered his private office together. All at once, without warning, Organized Crime Unit agents swarmed into Paul's club, wearing bulletproof vests, navy blue sweatshirts imprinted with *POLICE* in large white letters and OCU badges draped around their necks, weapons in hand.

Amid bright lights and chaos, Captain Charles Spencer imposed a distinctive feature as he approached David Coradini and directed him to assist in arresting the exotic dancers.

The club's customers were not the focus of the raid; they were ordered to leave at once and immediately complied. OCU agents were quick to spot packets of white powder on the floor, incriminating evidence of the club's ongoing drug activity.

Captain Patrick Lafferty had no previous knowledge about the impending bust. Overwhelmed, he sat in his parked car, watching the club's patrons as they hurriedly exited Lili's Cabaret.

Lafferty was in a quandary. He couldn't drive away; the area was surrounded by task force officers and their vehicles. Quickly thinking, he decided to act as though Lili's was on his routine patrol. Stepping out of his squad car, he approached the OCU agent outside the entrance and offered his assistance. The agent firmly shook his head. "We've got this situation under control. Just stay here—Captain Spencer will speak with you shortly."

The two FBI agents in the parking lot of the Mexican restaurant watched as the drama unfolded. They immediately radioed Agent Russell at headquarters, who directed them to offer assistance.

They rushed over to Lili's and walked through the cordoned-off area, flashing their badges. "FBI—we're here to lend support." They were quickly but politely advised that this was an Organized Crime Unit Operation under the jurisdiction of the Memphis Police Department. The rebuff was not well received and both agents turned and left the premises.

Two OCU officers emerged from Paul's office with Lou and Paul in handcuffs and announced to Captain Spencer, "There's a brown leather briefcase filled with money on the desk and an open safe containing a small amount of cocaine. Secure the area."

When Paul and Lou spotted David standing next to Captain Spencer with an *Organized Crime Unit* badge around his neck, they stared in shocked silence.

Paul's stunned look displayed disbelief that the David Coradini he had trusted was an undercover agent. Although Paul was providing payoffs to the police, he knew he couldn't make any deals with the OCU.

Lou remained wan and expressionless. He dreaded having to face his father, Gino.

Several minutes later, Captain Spencer approached Captain Lafferty, who immediately realized that David was with the OCU and could connect him to Lou Marchesino.

Spencer addressed Lafferty sharply. "You are implicated here and you will be subpoenaed. For now, you can go." He motioned to clear a path, after which Lafferty drove off quickly without saying a word.

After Lili's Cararet had been completely cleared, Captain Spencer and David secured the club's entrance with a steel chain and padlocked it.

Reporters and cameramen crowded the sidewalk as OCU officers began to leave and arrestees were escorted into police vans. The bust at Lili's Cabaret, with its Mafia owner, became a sensational news story. There was widespread speculation about the fate of several key players and their imminent encounter with justice.

The following morning, Henri Le Beau and Gino Marchesino flew to Memphis in their Citation.

John was seated in Chris' office in the Rawlins House, sipping coffee and reading the *Commercial Appeal's* account of the raid at Lili's when Chris returned from court. He had represented Paul Alfonso, Lou Marchesino and the club's dancers at their arraignments. Chris slowly poured himself a cup of coffee, recalling John's previous warning.

John set his paper aside. "Chris, I'm sorry that you're involved."

Heather, Chris' secretary, suddenly appeared in the doorway. She was a middle-aged professional dressed in business attire, with smartly-styled short brown hair and watchful blue eyes. Well versed in legal matters, Heather was an invaluable assistant to Chris. "Mr. Spencer, you have two visitors from New Orleans, Mr. Le Beau and Mr. Marchesino."

"Please ask them to come in," he replied.

Both men entered the office. After courteous introductions and handshakes, Heather offered them coffee. When they declined, she discreetly left the room. John, aware that Chris' visitors had come to discuss a legal matter, quickly excused himself.

Henri opened the conversation with a friendly gesture to Chris. "I am truly impressed. Your Rawlins House is beautiful. I thought that New Orleans offered the best historical houses, but I can see that you have a gem here in Memphis."

Chris, pleased by Henri's compliment, thanked him. He liked Henri's amiable Cajun personality. They had spoken the previous evening after Lou and Paul were arrested.

Henri spoke. "We appreciate what you've done. Let's address the business at hand. Gino is Lou's father. What are the charges?"

Chris responded firmly, "Lou has only one charge pending against him—cocaine. Paul has six charges. Bail has been set at five hundred thousand dollars for Lou, because he lives out of state, in Louisiana. The same amount is set for Paul. However," Chris pointed out, "they have a reliable witness who can testify against both, with incriminating evidence."

Henri asked immediately, "Who *is* this witness?"

Chris had an uncomfortable feeling. His father's words came to mind: *This is one client I wish you had turned down.*

Nonetheless, Chris knew that he was obliged to answer. "David Coradini—he's an undercover OCU agent."

Gino, who had been listening impassively, suddenly looked up. His eyes widened and he displayed an intense, icy expression as he bristled at the word "witness." It wasn't anything that Gino had said—it was what he *wasn't* saying. Chris intuitively sensed that Gino had no intention of letting this go.

Henri congenially intervened. "We'll arrange an attorney for Lou. At present, you are Paul's lawyer. We hope you will continue to assist in his defense, as well as his dancers." Chris unenthusiastically nodded in agreement.

Gino jumped up. "Let's go. Now! We'll post the bail."

Captain Spencer was at his OCU office, a nondescript brown brick building dating from the mid-Sixties, located one block from the Justice Complex. He was reviewing reports at his desk when two FBI agents, Dale Russell and Brad Barnett, were ushered in. Spencer politely invited them to sit down. The room was sparsely furnished—strictly for business—with only a file cabinet, desk and two straight-back chairs for visitors.

Russell spotted two framed pictures hanging on the wall—one a photograph of Charles Spencer in his Memphis police uniform; the other, a certificate bearing his name and *Organized Crime Unit*.

Smiling, Russell opened the conversation. "Captain Spencer, I must congratulate you on the OCU's arrests at Lili's Cabaret."

"I appreciate that," voiced Spencer.

Looking directly at Spencer, Russell continued. "Let me explain the FBI's role. We were quite aware that Lou Marchesino was handling the money for Carlos; however, we weren't ready to make our move, nor did we know about your undercover agent.

"You've got enough evidence on Paul Alfonso but not much on Lou Marchesino. This is what we should do: make this a federal case and use RICO. That would give us more clout against Lou."

Listening attentively, the captain replied, "You're right, but before we can go that route, certain steps need to be taken. I'll let you know tomorrow."

Russell reached over to shake hands with Spencer. Barnett, with an anxious voice, added, "I can assure you, timing is important. Gino will not wait."

The following afternoon, Gino and Lou sat in Alex LaCrosse's white Lincoln Town Car, parked near the OCU office. They were waiting to spot the undercover agent who could testify against Paul and Lou.

"*There* he is!" Lou suddenly exclaimed as he pointed to David Coradini. "He's with Captain Spencer and two other police officers. They're walking into the FBI building."

Gino sharply turned to Lou. "I expected this would happen. They're working together. You're in deeper than we thought."

Later that afternoon, three white Ford Fairlanes pulled out of the OCU garage in single file. Coradini was a passenger in the middle car. Gino and Lou began to follow the motorcade in their car. Once out of the downtown area, the OCU convoy began to speed up. Gino was careful not to follow too closely but wasn't worried about losing pursuit. He had received a tip from Captain Lafferty informing him that David was staying in a safe house—and the OCU vehicles were headed in that direction.

Gino drove slowly past the safe house, which was located in a quiet neighborhood on the outskirts of Memphis. He spotted two plainclothes guards on the porch and four unmarked vehicles parked in the yard, evidencing the presence of several others inside.

Gino looked at Lou. "We'll have to figure out some other way."

The following afternoon, with Paul Alfonso's file in a leather binder tucked under his arm, Captain Spencer arrived at the FBI's field office to confer with Agent Russell. The workplace was bustling with activity, with several agents sitting at their desks and others moving about, punctuated with the noise of typewriters and a ringing telephone. A few recognized Captain Spencer.

Dale Russell warmly greeted Spencer and ushered him into his private office, which was furnished with a dark walnut executive desk and chairs. They immediately proceeded to discuss the all-important documents.

Paul Alfonso had just arrived at Big Bob's, and Nina poured hot coffee for him and Joey. They moved to a table away from the crowded snack bar.

Paul tried to appear at ease, but couldn't conceal his tension. With a strained look, he confided to Joey, "I can't believe I hired an undercover agent!" He drew a deep breath of anger and disgust.

Joey nodded understandingly. "You're probably being watched, even coming here."

Paul shook his head. "No, I don't think so—but I'm not sure." Then, glancing around, he leaned forward and whispered in a low voice. "David Coradini, that OCU agent, is the only real witness against Lou and me." Paul gave Joey a sly look. "Gino assured me that he would take care of the problem."

In the FBI office, Agent Dale Russell and Captain Charles Spencer had been poring through Paul Alfonso's file for well over an hour. Agent Barnett suddenly appeared at the door. "We just received word—Paul Alfonso has been killed!" Russell and Spencer silently looked at each other in disbelief.

The shopping center at Big Bob's was swarming with police officers when Captain Spencer and Agent Russell arrived. The parking area had already been cordoned off with wide yellow tape displaying the words CRIME SCENE - DO NOT CROSS in bold, black letters.

Captain Patrick Lafferty of the Memphis Police Department was the officer in charge, directing the investigation. He immediately recognized Charles Spencer and Dale Russell as they approached the boundary tape. Lafferty walked over and waved them through. "Memphis Police have jurisdiction here. However, you're welcome."

Captain Lafferty, still retaining his position of authority, was cautiously extending a professional courtesy. He prudently avoided making any reference to the raid at Lili's Cabaret.

Lafferty escorted Spencer and Russell to where the body of Paul Alfonso lay upon the pavement. The door of his burgundy Cadillac Seville was open.

As Captain Spencer and Agent Russell leaned over the corpse, they observed two fatal wounds: one to the forehead;

one to the heart. Spencer recognized the *modus operandi* as a typical Mob-style execution.

"Who found him?" questioned Captain Spencer matter-of-factly.

"A woman in that parking lot," pointed Captain Lafferty. "She had just come out of the grocery store above Big Bob's and was wheeling her basket to her car when she spotted a body on the ground. She called out for help—we're still looking for other witnesses."

Several news reporters had already arrived at the crime scene, eager to cover the story. A crowd of onlookers gathered on the sidewalk behind the yellow tape. Among them were Joey Bellisario and Big Bob Drescher; both appeared shocked and dismayed.

Lafferty had already questioned Joey, who informed him that Paul had just left Big Bob's. Agent Russell politely asked, "Captain Lafferty, can you send photographs of the crime scene to the FBI? We would appreciate it."

"I can do that," Lafferty pleasantly responded, "but there's the ambulance. I'll have to go."

Walking to his car, Russell looked at Spencer. "The Marchesinos have a hand in this."

"There was enough evidence against Lou *with* Paul. Now," he added disappointedly, "there's not enough! To get Lou, we'll have to find some other way."

"I agree," echoed Spencer.

Suddenly, Russell's FBI radio crackled as the agent parked in the lot of Alex LaCrosse's air charter relayed news. "Gino and Lou Marchesino are getting ready to fly out of Memphis. Are there any orders?" he asked urgently.

"None," responded Russell bluntly. "There's nothing at the moment."

The silver Citation was soon winging through the blue skies, headed for New Orleans. Gino warned Lou, "You'd better lay low and stay out of trouble."

15

AT THE RAWLINS House office, John stared out the window at sporadic flashes of lightning, rolling thunder and a steady downpour of rain. Chris was on the phone, talking with a client who had been injured in an automobile accident.

John had spent several hours with Chris, disclosing his dealings with the Marchesinos.

At this point, Chris ended the call and addressed John.

"Now, where were we?" He paused patiently.

John slowly replied, "Let's go back to Patrick Lafferty."

"The Memphis Police commissioner was investigating Lafferty's connection to Lili's Cabaret and Lou Marchesino. There were rumors about Lafferty and his payoffs.

"Lafferty was worried," John added. "He knew he was entitled to a police hearing, but realizing that he was in deep trouble, he took his retirement immediately.

"After that, Chris, your father directed David Coradini with the OCU to hit all of Alfonso's clubs hard."

"I remember that, John. I was getting calls from irate club managers. That's when you and I went to visit the Lili's Cabarets."

AT THE WHITEHAVEN club, John and Chris noticed about twenty picketers walking back and forth on the sidewalk. The protesters were carrying large hand-lettered signs: *We don't want strip clubs here!* and *Get Religion.*

When Chris and John entered the club, they were confronted with an angry manager. He informed them that the OCU was checking drivers leaving the premises for alcohol and drugs, then making arrests.

Chris patiently waited until the manager finished complaining before responding. "Unfortunately, there's nothing I can do. The picketers and OCU officers are both within their rights."

Upon leaving the club, John and Chris made similar stops at other Lili's, then decided to visit Big Bob's to find out what was happening there.

Upon arriving, they found no picketers but observed two FBI agents in a brown Chevrolet that was conspicuously parked in front of Big Bob's. John thought, *They're doing exactly what they did at Mario's Bella Casa Country Club!*

After Joey and Big Bob greeted John and Chris, they all headed to the snack bar to order Nina's special hamburgers.

Joey wanted to know what was going on at the other clubs. Chris replied, "The OCU is trying to keep people away."

John observed that the usually busy bowling alley was almost empty; even the poolroom had just a few players.

Joey, aware of John's observation, voiced emphatically, "See what's happening, John? Paul Alfonso was murdered right outside our door! We're losing customers—they're afraid to come back!" Joey's anger increased. "Gino's behind this whole thing—he doesn't give a damn about Big Bob and me."

Alex LaCrosse arrived at Marchesino Enterprises to meet with Carlos and Henri; Alex had requested this meeting. Tina served small cups of espresso to each of them, save Henri, who instead requested a bottle of Perrier.

Alex was agitated and quickly got to the point. "Carlos, I provided a Lincoln for Henri and Gino while they were in Memphis. Henri returned to New Orleans, but Gino *didn't*—and he kept the car!"

"When I heard about Paul Alfonso, I suspected that it was Gino. If anyone spotted that car...." Alex hesitated. "The FBI will definitely investigate. Also, I saw two men with binoculars sitting inside an FBI car parked over in the FAA's lot. They were watching our business, Carlos. We have a major problem!"

Henri decisively added, "Alex is right. Let me tell you what the FBI is trying to do. They want to get Alex and Lou together, en route to New Orleans with illegal money." Henri paused. "Once they cross state lines, it becomes federal jurisdiction. They'll close LaCrosse Air Charter in a heartbeat! It'll hurt all of your casinos."

Carlos looked startled. Before he could respond, his face suddenly became pale and his eyes reflected acute pain. Carlos leaned back in his chair and held his hand to his heart, then hastily fumbled to remove a small pillbox from his coat pocket. Henri reacted quickly, knowing that Carlos carried nitroglycerin tablets. He handed Carlos his Perrier to drink with the medicine while Alex called for an ambulance.

After finishing the day's work, Janie sat with April in her den enjoying their favorite liqueur, Galliano.

"April," smiled Janie, "why don't you and I take a weekend vacation to Lake Tahoe when Dominic and John are both there? We would have a great time!"

April's eyes brightened. "That's a good idea. I could ask Dawn to handle things while I'm gone."

Suddenly, the telephone rang for the escort service. While April was engaged in the conversation, Janie walked over to the tall mahogany bookcase. She eyed several family photographs and a portrait of April's parents. Janie focused on April's mother, blonde and blue eyed, with her beaming smile.

Turning to April, who had just put down the phone, Janie pointed to the picture. "April, you told me that your mother died, but never said anything more."

April paused, then answered in a soft voice. "My father and I both loved my mother very much.

"She played an important role in my father's nightclub, the Bourbon Burlesque—charming the customers, hiring the right people and deciding who fit better in the other clubs.

"That was when I was in high school and my life was great." April smiled as she recalled the memory.

The smile quickly disappeared. "Then Gino came into the picture. He wanted drugs to be available in all the clubs because they were popular in the French Quarter and they made a lot of money.

"At first, my father wanted nothing to do with the drug business, but there was no way he could oppose Gino as underboss. He had no choice. Soon, my mother got involved. While she was making her usual delivery to one of the clubs, she was arrested by an undercover DEA agent.

"My father was angry and worried, realizing he was responsible—and that my mother faced prison. They didn't trust Gino. Those days were difficult for us.

"My mother just sat in our French Quarter apartment and," April paused, "that's where I found her."

Janie queried, "*Found* her?"

"Yes," she replied, "slumped in a chair with a needle on the floor beside her. The coroner said she had OD'd... a heroin overdose. Of course, the police were paid by the Family, so they went along with the report—but I didn't! My mother *never* used drugs."

April's voice was firm as she grew more incensed. "I always thought—and still do—that Gino was behind the whole thing. He wanted to be sure that no one could testify against him. I call it murder. I don't like Gino—and never will!"

"I'm so sorry," Janie said softly.

The telephone's sharp ring again interrupted their conversation. April answered. After a brief conversation, she turned to Janie with a stricken look. "That was my father. Carlos is in the hospital!"

The cardiologist informed Angela and Nicky that Carlos' heart attack was a warning. He must alter his stressful lifestyle or a second attack could be fatal.

John was sitting in Chris' office when Heather informed Chris, "There's a call for John from Nicky Marchesino."

John picked up the phone, listened and then said, "I'll be on my way."

Chris, noticing John's anxiety, asked, "What's wrong?"

"Carlos is ill," he replied. "Nicky needs me in Lake Tahoe immediately to take over for Dominic. He'll be leaving for New Orleans. Nicky is counting on me to help the new manager."

Chris looked worried. "John, you'd better be careful. The FBI is going to step up their investigation of Nicky and the casinos."

After spending several weeks in the hospital, Carlos was back home, recuperating. He was seated with Nicky in his armchair in the den without his favorite cigars—Angela had taken them away. Carlos was pondering what he should do. Nicky was taking care of the immediate business. However, other Marchesino Family members were speculating about Carlos' future.

With an anxious look, Carlos addressed Nicky. "I don't know if I can continue to effectively run this Family. By right, you are next in line—but if you refuse, I'll have to name Gino. I fear making that decision."

Nicky understood the dilemma facing his father: with Gino as Don, there would be more violence and killing. That mustn't happen!

"Father," stated Nicky, "I'm your son. I'll take your place if that's your wish. But I would run things my way."

Carlos nodded. "Yes, that is my wish. Do as you see fit." His eyes revealed great pride in his son, as he leaned back in relief.

Reaching over to his father, Nicky respectfully took Carlos' frail hand, and kissed his gold ring engraved with a magnificent face of a lion.

Realizing that he must inform Gino of his decision, Carlos invited him to their home the following afternoon.

Arriving at two o'clock, Gino was seated in the den with Carlos and Nicky. Suppressing emotion, Carlos looked at Gino. "I'm stepping down as Don. My son will take my place." Then, after pausing, "Gino, I hope that you approve."

Gino, sitting upright in his chair, was clearly displeased but remained impassive. Inwardly, he was livid and felt cheated; Carlos had chosen Nicky over him. Gino was convinced that his years of experience and stature made him a better candidate for Don. However, Nicky was Carlos' son.

Finally, he responded. "I accept your decision."

Nicky observed Gino's dark mood and immediately attempted to downplay his uncle's unspoken disappointment. "You are most competent, Gino. You'll have complete control of the gambling, all our strip clubs and brothels in Louisiana. However," Nicky stated firmly, "we're going to sell our Memphis strip clubs. The FBI is stepping up efforts against the Marchesinos there."

Gino spoke abruptly. "I can handle whatever needs to be done." Then he walked out. His departure was a rebuff, evident to both Carlos and Nicky. Gino had deliberately ignored the obligatory congratulations to Nicky and traditional kissing of the lion ring in honor of the new Don.

Dominic immediately proceeded to visit Nicky at Marchesino Enterprises. They were sharing conversation over small cups of steaming espresso with Sambuca when Nicky suddenly announced, "Dominic, I want you to be my underboss."

Dominic reacted with surprise. "I've always been with you, Nicky, and I'll continue but," he paused, "what about Gino? He won't take this lightly. He is Family."

Nicky listened. "I'm quite aware of how Gino feels."

Dominic continued forcefully. "Gino isn't going to do anything now, but if Carlos dies—and thank God he's doing well," Dominic quickly made the sign of the cross, "Gino will stop at nothing to get you and me out of the way. The young soldiers of the Family admire his bold way of enforcing. Gino will have their support."

Nicky pondered the thought, then looked earnestly at Dominic. "Carlos still represents authority and commands the respect of all Family members. Dominic, we'll deal with Gino when the time comes—but I need your answer now. If you don't want to be my underboss, I will accept your wish."

Dominic firmly answered without hesitation. "Of course I accept, Nicky. You knew I would."

The timbre of his voice validated his loyalty. They both rose from their chairs. Dominic hugged Nicky, then devotedly kissed his gold lion ring.

The weather was sunny and warm, and April was in a joyful mood as she prepared to meet Dominic for a late midday lunch in the French Quarter. Her office was closed, as Janie had arranged to spend the afternoon with a business client in Kenner.

April sat with Dominic at a wrought-iron table underneath a bright red awning at their favorite bistro, Barletta's, as they ate fried oyster po' boy sandwiches.

Dominic looked worried and his mood was sullen. He had unpleasant news for April but had to tell her. "My duties as underboss are only with Nicky. Gino is now in charge of all the New Orleans businesses—and that includes your escort service, April. That means you'll have to deal with Gino."

April looked aghast. "I don't believe this! Can't you do something?" she asked pleadingly.

"I can help you get out of the escort business. Let someone else run it. You have enough money, April." Dominic then offered encouragement. "You're a talented and resourceful person. There are so many other things you could do—like opening a fashion boutique, a souvenir shop or whatever else you want." He tried to make April understand that he didn't want her to deal with Gino.

An uncomfortable silence followed. Quite unexpectedly, April threw down her po' boy and blurted out, "I don't like this!" Pushing her chair back and standing up, she added in a hurt voice, "Dominic, you've disappointed me." Onlookers stared as she briskly walked out.

Dominic sat there, stunned. Looking around, he was keenly aware that several customers at nearby tables had noticed the unpleasant scene and recognized who he was.

Chris heard nothing from Henri LeBeau after the case against Lou Marchesino was dropped. Then one Monday morning, Henri called to inform Chris that he was coming to Memphis.

When Henri arrived at the Rawlins House, he was soon seated comfortably. Chris was greatly relieved that Gino hadn't accompanied him; he had been considering how he could distance himself from Paul Alfonso's business dealings. It was a delicate subject that Chris wasn't anxious to broach.

"I'm here at Nicky Marchesino's request," announced Henri. Noticing Chris' inquisitive look, Henri explained. "Surely you've heard that Carlos has stepped down and that Nicky is now Don. He's been busy with Family matters, but it's Nicky's decision to terminate all of the Marchesinos' business in Memphis as soon as possible. After that, your legal services will no longer be required. Of course," Henri smiled, "we may need to consult you again in the future. You *will* be available, I presume?"

"I'll try to do whatever I can," Chris replied politely.

Henri continued. "You may inform Captain Spencer of our intention." Henri's charming but disarming approach had an underlying purpose. He knew that, by sharing this information, the FBI would also be informed. Henri then thanked Chris for his services and departed.

Chris telephoned his father, who immediately notified Agent Russell. "Yes, we've heard. Our FBI agents in New Orleans have already stepped up surveillance on the Marchesinos."

Friday afternoon, after her scene at the French Quarter bistro, April was in the den sipping a Galliano with Janie. April's mood was downcast. She confided to Janie why she and Dominic were at odds. Janie understood that this separation not only made April sad, but also uneasy about Gino coming to her house. The telephone suddenly rang.

Janie knew about April's escort service although she never inquired about any details. However, she was aware that weekends meant business.

"Yes, eight p.m.... one hundred dollars... credit card." Janie had picked up snippets of April's brief conversation and, after the call, she questioned April. "What about this escort business? How does it work?"

April expressed surprise at her question, but casually responded, "I collect the one hundred dollar fee for *using* the service."

Noticing Janie's curious look, she added, "You've met Dawn next door; once she's contacted, I have no further involvement. Dawn arranges the dates and the charges, which vary based on the girl and the activity.

"That last caller is a regular. No doubt, he'll pay a high price, maybe five hundred dollars, to spend the evening with one of Dawn's youngest girls. He likes a pretty, fresh face that isn't overly made-up. She'll probably dress up as a cheerleader to remind him of when he was a teenager.

"As for Dawn's other women, the date could involve a night of elegant entertainment or something else—maybe black leather, handcuffs and whips. It all depends on what the client wants."

Janie looked astonished, "Wow! I had no idea."

April cracked a tiny smile. "Dawn and her girls make good money, but the Marchesinos take a percentage of what the house makes—that's understood. Dominic used to make the pickups here. I was never worried, but now that Gino's taking Dominic's place..." April's voice became disquieting, "I have a bad feeling about this.

"Maybe I should get out of the escort business. Dominic wants me to, but Dawn is my friend. I'll really have to think about it."

April anxiously watched Janie. "Could you be here early on Monday, before Gino comes to get the money? There's something about Gino that scares me—and I really don't want to be alone with him!"

"Of course, April," replied Janie. "I'm glad to be here for you."

Monday morning was a typical New Orleans day: hot and humid. When the doorbell chimed, April admitted Gino and Lou. Janie positioned herself in her office doorway, making a point of being conspicuously visible.

Gino was cordial and immediately introduced his son, Lou, who eyed Janie with interest. They both knew about her affair with Nicky. Janie responded to the introduction politely but coolly.

Gino addressed April. "I'm still in charge, but Lou will make these pickups for me from now on." April simply nodded and handed Lou a sizable envelope. She was anxious to complete today's business.

Quite unexpectedly, Lou opened the envelope and started counting the money. Smiling broadly, he glanced at Gino. "Three thousand dollars."

Suddenly, an FBI agent in an unmarked van parked a short distance away shouted, "It's the money. We've got 'em!" The FBI had installed listening devices in April's home the day that she lunched with Dominic at the bistro and Janie was away from her office for the afternoon. Using high-frequency receivers, headphones and tape recorders, they had monitored every conversation since.

Agents Russell and Barnett immediately gave the signal to a team of four, who were wearing navy blue sweatshirts with *FBI* blazoned in big, yellow letters. With guns drawn, they quickly burst through the front door of April's house, seizing the envelope that April had just given to Lou.

With a grin, Russell confirmed, "The money." Lou understood what that meant. Russell then ordered the arrests of Gino, Lou, April and Janie.

Everyone was routinely searched. In a clear voice, Russell informed all four of their Miranda rights. "You have the right to remain silent. Anything you say can and will be used against you in a court of law."

April was dazed; she couldn't believe what was happening. Lou displayed a defiant expression. Janie remained silent but noticed that Gino stared accusingly in April's direction. He said nothing but his glaring eyes reflected anger.

Agent Russell had not fully anticipated the outcome. Initially, they had intended to snare Dominic, who was making the money pickups. However, Russell was extremely gratified to have apprehended Gino and Lou.

At the New Orleans FBI office, Agent Russell was preparing to question April Giovanetti. He was direct. "There were FBI listening devices hidden in your residence. We heard you explain how the escort service and the house next door are run."

"We went after the escort service to get the Marchesinos. We've got sufficient evidence." Russell's tone now became brusquer. "You'll go to prison unless you cooperate with us. We'll drop the charges against you if you testify against Gino and Lou Marchesino. Ms. Giovanetti, it's *your* decision."

Russell waited patiently for the pathetic young woman sitting before him to reply.

April closed her eyes for a moment and slowly shook her head. Hesitating, she finally responded in a clear, steady voice. "No; I can't testify. Do you know what they'll do to me? They'll kill me! I'd rather go to prison."

Russell quickly assured her. "We could enroll you in the Federal Witness Protection Program and you could start a new life somewhere far from New Orleans. We'll make sure that you are safe."

Before April could respond, there was a sharp knock on the door. Brad Barnett announced, "Ms. Giovanetti's attorney, Henri Le Beau, just arrived."

Russell nodded, then addressed April. "Think about everything I've said."

April was relieved to be home. Janie was with her. April and Dominic's deep affection for each other overshadowed their misunderstanding. Dominic realized that his involvement with Nicky's business matters had caused him to overlook the FBI's surveillance of April's house. He felt guilty about this.

Janie was chatting with April in her sunny kitchen and sipping a cup of café au lait when Dominic entered. He had called an electronics expert, who was methodically checking each room with a "sweeper," a radio frequency detector designed to locate all of the FBI's listening devices.

Dominic held up two tiny, shiny objects. "This bug," he announced, "was in the ceiling fan of the living room."

"Right where Gino and Lou were standing," affirmed Janie.

"But, that's not the only one. This one was in your den, April, in your antique clock."

Janie's face paled. "The den! April, we were in the den when I asked you about the escort service. I am so sorry—it's my fault."

April quickly reassured her. "Janie, this *isn't* your fault. I should've realized that this could happen."

With a determined voice, Dominic interrupted. "I promise you, we'll work this out. I'll make sure of it."

16

NICKY HAD BEEN Don for only a few weeks when he requested a meeting with Dominic, Henri Le Beau, Gino and Lou to discuss the arrests at April's house. He knew that a difficult task lay before him.

Henri began with a pleasant smile. "This isn't as drastic as it seems. I'm working to suppress admission of the tape transcripts as evidence, which would make the arrests illegal. If we're successful, there would be no case. If that doesn't work, I'm confident that we can settle this with the Department of Justice without too much trouble—and little or no prison time. That's all I can tell you at the moment." Henri appeared confident and waited for a response.

Lou appeared satisfied.

Gino remained unconvinced by Henri's positive remarks and challenged Henri in a sharp tone. "I'm aware of the legal maneuvering when someone has incriminating evidence. I don't believe these charges will be so easily settled. There are *witnesses* who will be called against Lou and me. That cannot happen." Gino was adamant.

Upon hearing Gino's alarming words, Dominic angrily rose from his seat before Henri could respond. "You may be right, Gino, but no matter what, *nothing* must happen to April!"

Nicky, observing the hostility between Dominic and Gino, quickly asserted, "I agree with Dominic." Looking at Gino, Nicky issued a firm ultimatum. "You will not harm *anyone*! Do you understand?" Nicky was also thinking of Janie.

In a more placating tone, Nicky continued. "Gino, let's not jump to conclusions. Henri is very competent—he'll work this out!"

With an icy glare, Gino quickly rose and left the conference room, accompanied by Lou.

Henri addressed Nicky with a dejected tone. "Gino is going to be difficult to deal with."

April's escort service had closed and many of Janie's interior design customers were calling to cancel their appointments. April often joined Janie to talk over a Galliano. "I'm so very sorry." Then, angrily, "What was Lou trying to prove by counting that money? He's the one who put us all in jeopardy!"

The doorbell chimed and Dominic quickly stepped inside, hugging April tightly. Janie could sense the deep emotion drawing them together.

Upon seeing Janie, Dominic addressed her. "I'm glad you're here. I have a message for you. Nicky needs to see you—now."

Nicky was waiting when Janie arrived at Marchesino's office. Her eyes twinkling, she spoke with a bright smile. "So *you* are the Don. That doesn't surprise me." She had already spotted the gold lion ring on Nicky's finger.

Nicky was surprised by Janie's remark, recalling that he had once confided to her that he never wanted to head the Family. He answered, "I really didn't have a choice."

He transitioned to a more businesslike tone. "Henri Le Beau has advised me that you'll be subpoenaed as a witness for the trials of April, Gino and Lou."

Janie simply nodded as Nicky continued. "There's no case against you, Janie, but the prosecution will try to get you to talk about April's escort business and the brothel next door.

"Dominic is at April's now. She's going to Nakoma Vista this evening and she'll stay there until her court date."

Nicky didn't elaborate but he was quite firm. "I'd like you to go to Lake Tahoe with April. Dominic and I don't trust Gino—or Lou. We think both of you will be safer in Tahoe. The guards at Nakoma Vista Casino can't allow Gino or Lou to enter. It's just a necessary precaution."

Janie thought, then responded, "I'll go to Tahoe."

Nicky appeared greatly relieved. "Our plane will fly you and April out tonight."

Janie reached over to hug him, then smiled. "Now, should I kiss your ring?"

Nicky laughed.

Janie returned to her apartment on La Rue Charité to hurriedly pack her suitcases. She decided to call John to let him know that she was coming to Lake Tahoe.

Hearing Janie's voice on the telephone was a complete surprise to John. "April and I are coming to Lake Tahoe late tonight. We're looking forward to a long visit!" Janie was excited but didn't explain further.

John's thoughts were racing. *What's this all about? How is Janie able to leave her business? What about April? Dominic isn't here at Nakoma Vista.* It didn't make sense. John knew that something was wrong.

April's trust in Dominic was implicit. She understood why she had to leave New Orleans. Her blue eyes reflected her happiness as she and Dominic were lying in a warm embrace in her pink bedroom. Time seemed floatingly endless.

April abruptly broke the silence. "Dominic, Janie will be here soon. I need to shower and dress—and I haven't even started packing! I'm hungry, too. We'll have to eat something before we leave. Why don't you go to Romano's and bring back a pizza?"

Dominic hesitated. He didn't want to leave April, even for a little while.

April smiled. "Order us a large sausage and pepperoni with onions and extra cheese. Hurry—please!"

Reluctantly, Dominic agreed, hugged her and gave her a parting kiss. "I'll only be gone for thirty minutes."

Stepping out of her red Mustang convertible, Janie glanced up at threatening dark clouds, hoping that their flight to Tahoe wouldn't encounter stormy weather. As she began walking toward April's gate, she spotted a black car quickly pulling away.

Anxiously, Janie ran up the stone steps to find the front door slightly ajar. It wasn't like April to leave the house open. Janie quietly entered the hallway, where she encountered an eerie silence that made her more uncomfortable.

Janie called out, "April!" There was no answer. Her heart beat rapidly as she hurried up the stairs.

When she reached the bedroom, Janie found April on the floor, her blonde hair streaked with blood; her body lifeless.

Janie knelt beside April, shaking with tears streaming down her face. She cried out as if expecting a response. "Oh my God! April, what happened?"

Upon returning, Dominic heard Janie's frantic voice and, within seconds, appeared in the doorway of April's bedroom. With a single glance, he saw April lying on the floor.

Kneeling and sobbing, Dominic gently took April in his arms. *If only he hadn't left!*

After several minutes, Dominic silently rose and helped Janie up. Looking at him with a pained expression, she sputtered, "I saw something—a black car—two men—driving away."

Dominic stiffened, his face bearing a stony look. He *knew*—Gino owned a black Mercedes Benz. He immediately called Nicky.

Lieutenant Jean Deveraux with the New Orleans Police Department promptly arrived at April's house upon receiving Nicky's telephone call. Deveraux was in charge of the case. He was a short, husky Cajun, in his sixties, with probing dark eyes and graying hair—and well-liked by the Marchesino Family.

The lieutenant observed that the victim had been shot twice, in the head and the heart. Recognizing the *modus operandi*, he knew that a mob hitman was often never found. Occasionally, the police were successful in making an arrest—usually someone with a long rap sheet or a heroin addict of little consequence.

Deveraux pondered. *This situation is different. Nicky Marchesino called me because he and Dominic believe that Gino did this.*

Deveraux suspected that Gino Marchesino was behind many unsolved murders. He thought, *Perhaps this time, Gino will finally be held accountable.*

The crime scene was carefully marked, with evidence and numerous photographs taken. The coroner was removing April's body from the upstairs bedroom as Lieutenant Deveraux completed his initial investigation.

April's house on La Rue Dauphine was cordoned off with familiar yellow tape. News of April Giovanetti's death spread quickly and a throng of spectators and reporters was already gathering in the street. Pouring rain added to the dismal night. Dominic, holding a black umbrella, escorted Janie to his Lincoln. They quickly drove away.

FBI Agents Russell and Barnett were waiting to speak with Lieutenant Deveraux. "I know he works with the Marchesinos," Russell stated to his partner. "He won't tell us anything, but he can't refuse our request for crime scene photos."

"Our case is seriously compromised now—*unless* we can convince Janie Fox to help us."

Janie leaned back in her car seat and asked Dominic, "Will you take me to my apartment on La Rue Charité?"

Dominic agreed, then assured her, "Tomorrow you'll fly to Lake Tahoe."

"No," said Janie. Her eyes were brimming with tears. "I can't go then! Not until after April's funeral."

Dominic didn't persist. "I'll talk to Nicky. He knows how much you loved April. He's just looking out for your safety." He then added, "I'll have guards posted right away for your protection."

Once inside her apartment, Janie was immediately on the telephone with John, sobbing and whispering. "Please come! April is dead. I really need you here."

John was speechless—stunned—but pulled himself together and assured Janie, "I'll be there as soon as I can."

Upon receiving the urgent call, Alex LaCrosse informed John, "We'll have our plane ready to leave Lake Tahoe tomorrow at six a.m. That's the best I can do."

John couldn't sleep that night. When he left for the Lake Tahoe Airport, it was not yet daylight, but darkness soon began to recede, with a faint golden glow on the eastern horizon. Before long, the Gulfstream was winging through the early morning sky, en route to New Orleans.

John's thoughts focused on Janie. *Is she safe? Nothing must happen to her! Will I be able to protect her from danger?* He had packed his .38 Special revolver, just in case.

FBI Agent Russell immediately went to see Janie Fox. When he and Brad Barnett pulled up at her apartment on La Rue Charité, they were spotted by two men in a dark blue Buick Riviera who were carefully eyeing them. Russell recognized them as Marchesino bodyguards and drove away.

With a perturbed voice, he addressed Barnett. "Looks like the Marchesinos have recognized that Ms. Fox is a valuable commodity. We'll have to figure out a different approach. At least we know that Janie Fox is being protected."

Several guards were already posted at the Marchesino estate. Gino had made his position clear.

Dominic was sitting on the veranda of Nicky's white bungalow, drinking his breakfast coffee. He suddenly put his cup down and addressed Nicky harshly. "I warned Gino—and so did you!" His eyes imparted a steely gleam. "I won't let him get away with April's murder."

Nicky calmly reassured him. "Dominic, Devereaux will get Gino. If he doesn't, I won't stand in your way."

Just then, Lieutentant Deveraux called. He had arrived with three other police officers at Gino's Metairie residence. "Gino isn't here," he stated, "but I'm leaving two of my men to watch. We'll find him!"

There was a dark stillness at Marchesino Enterprises. Tina had already heard about April's tragic murder. She was busying herself at her desk when Lou Marchesino came in. Tina and Lou were distant cousins and had known each other since childhood. Lou had a way about him, always flirting with Tina. She appreciated his flattering compliments, but today, Lou was abrupt. "Tina, I need to contact Janie Fox. You have her apartment address in your Rolodex, right?"

Tina remained composed but conflicting thoughts ran through her mind. *Why does Lou need to talk to Janie right now—especially at her apartment? This doesn't quite add up. I wish Nicky was here.* Nonetheless, Lou was a Marchesino; Tina had no choice but to give him Janie's address.

Lou drove his black Mercedes to a neighborhood café located just beyond the Garden District. He spotted Gino sitting at a small table and handed him a piece of paper. Gino nodded but said nothing. He had no remorse and believed that his motives were justifiable. The tide of recent events had created uncertainty among the Marchesinos. Looking directly at Lou, Gino spoke in a subdued tone, "As soon as we take care of this, we'll go to Carlos and he'll work everything out."

Upon arriving in New Orleans, John took a taxi from Lakefront Airport to Janie's apartment. When he rang the bell, two muscular young men wearing black shirts and pants quickly appeared at John's side, demanding, "Why are you here? Identify yourself!"

Before John could reply, Janie opened the security door and nodded to the Marchesino bodyguards that John was okay.

Once inside the hallway, they embraced. Seated by the bubbling fountain in the sunny courtyard, Janie sadly informed John about April.

Tina was sitting at her desk when Nicky and Dominic entered the office. "Thank God, you're here!" she declared with a worried expression. "Something isn't right. Lou just stopped by and asked for Janie's address."

"Did you give it to him?" he snapped.

"I had to," she replied.

Alarmed, Nicky ordered Tina to call Lieutenant Deveraux at the New Orleans police station. "Tell him to go to 875 La Rue Charité, apartment number one, immediately. Tell him it's urgent! Dominic and I are on our way."

Resuming their watch at Janie's apartment, Marchesino's bodyguards were suddenly distracted when two scantily clad, attractive women strolled by. One was a buxom platinum blonde. "She looks like Jayne Mansfield," commented one of the bodyguards. "You're right, she does," his partner agreed. Waving coquettishly, the street-walkers approached the parked car.

In that solitary moment of diversion, the two unsuspecting bodyguards failed to recognize the danger. It was too late!

John and Janie were sitting quietly in the courtyard when they suddenly heard what sounded like gunshots from the street. Looking up, they saw Gino and Lou at the iron security door, trying to get inside. Janie became extremely frightened and panicked.

John rose and quickly grabbed her. "Come on! We have to get inside your apartment. Hurry!"

As they rushed inside, Tina was calling the New Orleans Police Department with Nicky's message. Summoned by the Marchesinos, Lieutenant Deveraux and his partner were dutifully en route within minutes.

Janie, white-faced and frozen with fear, stood inside her little apartment in John's protective arms. Her whole world had suddenly collapsed.

For the first time, Janie confronted a hidden truth: *I've always depended on John. He's been there for me no matter what. And now I've drawn him into my perilous plight without ever considering the consequences!*

With a look of desperation, Janie reached up and kissed John tenderly. "Why have I waited so long to tell you that I love you? I always have."

John hugged her tightly. "Janie, without you, there's no life for me. But this isn't the time to talk about regrets."

He tried to smile reassuringly, "Go into your bedroom and lock the door. You'll be safe there."

John knew that this was a fleeting sanctuary. Within a minute, Gino and Lou arrived at Janie's apartment door, kicking it loudly. A few seconds later, they fired several gunshots and shattered the lock. This should have allowed entry, but strangely, the door didn't give way. Somehow, the sturdy overhead latch held fast. With several more blows, however, Gino and Lou would be inside Janie's apartment.

When Lieutenant Deveraux and his partner arrived at 875 La Rue Charité, they spotted a Buick parked across the street. They discovered two men inside, shot at close range. Both of Janie's bodyguards were dead.

Drawing their weapons, Deveraux and his partner immediately proceeded to the apartment. Observing that the lock on the outer security door had been shot off, they cautiously entered the pathway leading to the inner courtyard, where they heard pounding and kicking at the door. Despite their stealthy approach, Lou was quick to hear them. Turning around, he aimed and fired several times. Deveraux's partner fell to the ground, mortally wounded.

Instinctively, with deadly aim, Lieutenant Deveraux retaliated, killing Lou. Gino returned fire several times and struck Deveraux, who helplessly fell to the ground, dropping his gun.

Gino bent over his son and saw that Lou was lifeless. He couldn't believe that Lou was dead, but he could see that Lieutenant Deveraux was moving. Gino was determined to avenge his son's death. "I'll kill you," he said aloud as he prepared to deliver the *coup de grâce*.

Before he could act, Gino heard footsteps. Wheeling around, he recognized John. With unwavering eyes focused on him, he pointed his .38-caliber handgun.

Gino saw John's look of cold determination and suddenly faced reality. He mumbled with a contemptuous tone, "So *you* are Memphis John."

John defiantly answered, "That's my name."

There was a moment of deadly silence.

John fired three quick shots. Gino was dead before he hit the ground.

Nicky and Dominic suddenly arrived at the apartment and immediately inventoried the scene, discovering that both Gino and Lou were dead.

Dominic replaced his gun in his shoulder holster.

Nicky stared quietly at Lieutenant Deveraux as John and Janie tried to stem the bleeding from his wound.

Lieutenant Deveraux looked up at Nicky, weak but able to speak. "My partner and Lou are dead. Gino tried to kill me." His voice became raspy. "John came out of that apartment. He killed Gino."

Nicky didn't react at first—he couldn't believe what he heard. Yet he had to admit that Gino was no longer his problem. Nevertheless, as a Marchesino, he would act accordingly.

Nicky spoke in a firm voice, "John, go! Now! Before police backup arrives. And Janie, you too. I'll handle things here.

Leave! Both of you." Then he addressed John. "I'll be in touch with you."

April was buried next to her mother. Her father, Dominic and Nicky gathered together at the gravesite. A few of April's close friends, including Dawn, stood nearby, as did John with a tearful Janie.

After the service, they quickly headed to the airport.

AT THE RAWLINS House office, Chris leaned forward in his chair with an incredulous look. "You killed Gino! Won't the Marchesinos come after you?"

"No, Chris. Nicky worked things out so Lieutenant Deveraux was the one who shot both Gino and Lou in self-defense. Nothing further developed—and nothing ever will."

Chris exclaimed, "I can't believe what I'm hearing!" Just then, the telephone rang and Chris announced, "Sharon will be here in a few minutes. Janie's with her."

John was reflective.

17

UPON THEIR RETURN to Memphis, Janie moved into John's River Bluff condominium. She needed time to digest and reconcile the traumatic events in New Orleans that had forever altered her life and ended April's. Janie felt that John had always cared for her and sought his solace in the long months that followed. Slowly, her emotional scars began to heal.

John and Janie spent many evenings on the Riverbluff Walkway, cherishing their time together. They fondly recalled the lazy days they had spent at their favorite retreat atop the river bluff, faded yet comforting memories from a time so long ago. They watched spectacular sunsets and the stars and moon that lit the panoramic night sky.

On a warm and sunny Saturday afternoon, Janie and John walked along the Riverbluff Walkway until they reached an overlook not far from their condo. As they paused, John looked down at the Church of the River. "Janie, don't you remember how we always liked to go there?"

"Look at the cars! Must be a wedding," Janie smiled, pointing.

When she turned back, she saw John on one knee. He was holding a ring for Janie to see. Gazing intently, he picked up her hand and slowly said, "I love you, Janie. I've always loved you and I want you to marry me. Will you?"

Without hesitation, Janie's words came. "Yes—yes, John, I will. I want to be with you"

John placed the ring on Janie's finger. Then he kissed her.

JOHN AND JANIE were married in the Church of the River overlooking the Mississippi. Their wedding day arrived with a warm sun and soft September breeze.

Janie was a radiantly beautiful bride. Sharon, as the matron of honor, helped Janie to select a long, white silk gown, elegantly simple and trimmed with Alençon lace. Janie entwined a crown of tiny pink rosebuds in her dark hair.

John, with Chris as his best man, stood at the altar, filled with a long-awaited happiness.

Their wedding was attended by family and a select group of close friends. The newlyweds, with the Foxes and Harrisons, greeted their well-wishers in the reception hall after the ceremony. Brent Fox wore a beaming smile, and for good reason—Janie was finally home!

Harriet accompanied the Foxes. "Can't miss my baby's wedding!" she voiced.

The guests enjoyed hors d'oeuvres and a buffet dinner that included tossed salad, sautéed vegetables, prime rib, salmon and fettuccine. The music was provided by Tyrone Jones Entertainment.

William Reese congratulated the couple, as did Charles Spencer, who joined Joey and Big Bob at the buffet table. Aware that Joey had phased out gambling and bookmaking, Captain Spencer reached out cordially to shake extended hands.

John and Janie settled into their River Bluff condominium. John continued to work in real estate, with legal assistance from Chris. However, Janie showed little interest in interior design—it was a painful reminder of April. John also harbored regrets. *If only I had never met the Marchesinos....*

UPON ENTERING CHRIS' office, Sharon brightly announced, "It's been raining all day. Janie and I couldn't do much, but it's let up now. We're ready to get something to eat. Let's all go to the Rendezvous!"

"Sounds good to me," said John.

Chris observed Janie studying the youthful portrait of Maggie and quietly asked, "Do you like it?"

"Yes," Janie replied with a wistful smile. "I can picture Maggie as a true Southern Belle—a plantation home, rose garden, oak trees and a wide veranda with a porch swing—a place where she can visit with her friends and enjoy a few mint juleps."

"I like that," laughed Chris.

Picking up on their conversation, John suggested, "Janie, you always loved to paint. Why don't you take it up again?"

"I think I will," she answered with an airy lilt in her voice.

The harsh ringing of the telephone abruptly interrupted the pleasure of this moment. When Chris answered, he bore a startled expression. Placing his hand over the receiver, he spoke in a calm voice, "John, it's for you—Nicky Marchesino!"

There was a sudden stillness as John slowly picked up the telephone.

I was afraid this would happen. Every time that Las Vegas reporter shows up at Nakoma Vista, Nicky expects me to be there to welcome guests. That's what he says—but what he actually wants is for me to maintain the legitimacy of his casino as its nominal owner. Will this ever end? Besides, like Jimmy Hoffa, Max Massey will never be found. I wonder, where does that leave me?

END

Made in the USA
Monee, IL
27 August 2020